**Up ahead, she could see the final turnoff to the road leading to the Hitching Post. In just minutes, they would call off their engagement, as planned.**

Admitting the engagement couldn't be real, that she had no hope left for a chance with Mitch, made her feel empty inside. The feeling only confirmed what she had known from the minute she had seen him again. She had always loved him.

But now, she needed to walk away.

When they reached the hotel and he began to turn his truck toward the parking area, she said, "Just drop me off in front, please."

He kept driving. "I'm not letting you go in to break the news to your family on your own."

"It's all right—"

"Not by me, it isn't."

"I can handle it, Mitch."

"It was my idea that got you into this," he said stubbornly. "Besides, I'm going to have to face your family sometime, too. I might as well do it now." He parked the truck and took her overnight bag from the rear seat.

She would always regret this morning.

But she could never forget last night.

Dear Reader,

One of the many things I love about the writing home I've found here is I'm able to share my favorite kind of stories with you. Small towns and families. Softhearted yet strong heroines. Sexy and even stronger heroes. Quirky but sometimes interfering characters. When I settle down to write—or to read—a book, those story elements are at the top of my list. I hope they're favorites for you, too.

*The Lawman's Christmas Proposal* has all of the above, along with Grandpa Jed up to his matchmaking tricks again and the entire town joining in on some holiday fun. Enjoy this visit to Cowboy Creek!

I always love to hear from you, so please feel free to get in touch through my website, barbarawhitedaille.com, or mailing address, PO Box 504 Gilbert, AZ 85299. You can also find me on Facebook and Twitter.

All my best to you.

Until we meet again,

*Barbara White Daille*

# THE LAWMAN'S CHRISTMAS PROPOSAL

BARBARA WHITE DAILLE

HARLEQUIN® AMERICAN ROMANCE®

Recycling programs
for this product may
not exist in your area.

ISBN-13: 978-0-373-75596-7

The Lawman's Christmas Proposal

Copyright © 2015 by Barbara White-Rayczek

This edition published by arrangement with Harlequin Books S.A.

For questions and comments about the quality of this book, please contact us at CustomerService@Harlequin.com.

**Printed in U.S.A.**

**Barbara White Daille** and her husband still inhabit their own special corner of the wild, wild Southwest, where the summers are long and hot and the lizards and scorpions roam.

Barbara loves looking back at the short stories and two books she wrote in grade school and realizing that—except for the scorpions—she's doing exactly what she planned. She has now hit double digits with published novels and still has a file drawer full of stories to be written.

As always, Barbara hopes you will enjoy reading her books! She would love to have you drop by her website for a visit, barbarawhitedaille.com.

## Books by Barbara White Daille

### Harlequin American Romance

*The Sheriff's Son*
*Court Me, Cowboy*
*Family Matters*
*A Rancher's Pride*
*The Rodeo Man's Daughter*
*Honorable Rancher*
*Rancher at Risk*

### The Hitching Post Hotel Series

*The Cowboy's Little Surprise*
*A Rancher of Her Own*

### Texas Rodeo Barons

*The Texan's Little Secret*

Visit the Author Profile page
at Harlequin.com for more titles.

To all my readers,
thank you for your support,
and Happy Holidays—no matter
which ones you celebrate!

And of course, to my number one reader, Rich.

# *Prologue*

"Don't look now, but here comes trouble," Jedediah Garland said to his old friend Paz.

He had driven her into town to pick up a food order for the Hitching Post, the hotel he owned and where she worked as his cook. On the way, they had made a quick stop for coffee at SugarPie's, Cowboy Creek's popular sandwich shop. As usual at this early hour, they found the place filled to capacity.

The woman approaching their table owned SugarPie's, which consisted of both the shop and the adjacent bakery.

Paz looked over her shoulder, then turned back. "Why do you say trouble, Jed? Sugar is smiling."

"That she is. And that smile's telling me she's got something more than today's menu on her mind. Haven't you?" he asked as the woman came to a halt beside their table. He gestured to an empty chair. "Take a seat, and let's hear whatever load of gossip you've got for us this morning."

Sugar grinned at him. She plopped into a pink-cushioned chair beside Paz, who scooted her chair over to allow the sturdy businesswoman a little more elbow room.

"Now, Jed," Sugar said in her soft Southern drawl, "how did you ever know I had something to say?"

He shrugged. "That not-so-sugar-sweet smile on your face is a dead giveaway." He crossed his arms over his chest. "Let's have it."

"Well…" After a quick look around the crowded shop, she leaned forward and said, "Lyle stopped in this morning."

Jed nodded, knowing she meant Lyle Weston, Cowboy Creek's sheriff.

"Is there something wrong?" Paz asked.

Sugar shook her head. "No. Well…there is and there isn't. Mitch is home."

Attention caught, Jed leaned forward. "Home? You mean to stay?"

Sugar shrugged. "Lyle doesn't know for sure himself. But he'll settle for having the boy here till the holidays."

No wonder the woman had been grinning like a fool. Mitch was the sheriff's oldest son, now an officer with the Los Angeles Police Department. While Lyle was fit to bust with pride over all the boy's commendations, no one in town liked the idea of him living so far away.

Trouble was, nobody knew what had been to blame for Mitch's departure. And at the moment, Jed didn't know what had led to the boy's return.

One of the waitresses signaled to Sugar from over near the kitchen. She hustled away, leaving Jed and Paz staring at each other.

"Oh, Jed," Paz said in a low voice. "I know that look. You're at it again."

His grin must have rivaled Sugar's, and no doubt Paz had accurately read his mind.

A self-proclaimed matchmaker, he'd had some success bringing two of his granddaughters together with the men meant for them. "Well, why not?" he demanded. "The Christmas season's almost upon us—and isn't that the time for miracles? Besides, no sense putting myself out to pasture when I'm on a winning streak on the track. *And* when I've got one granddaughter still unattached."

"But, Jed...you can't think Andi is ready for a relationship yet."

"I don't think she knows what she's ready for." He looked down at his coffee cup rather than meet Paz's eyes. He couldn't admit she had a point.

As her gaze caught his again, the tears in her eyes told him he didn't have to confess a thing. She was as much a part of his family as Tina, the granddaughter they shared and who was now happy and settled, thanks to their efforts.

Paz knew as well as he did that the entire family feared his widowed granddaughter, Andi, would never be happy again.

# Chapter One

*Two days later*

With the finesse of a well-trained pickpocket, Mitch Weston snagged a carrot from the vegetable tray his mother was preparing. Of course, a skilled pickpocket wouldn't have been dumb enough to flash the stolen goods—at least, not until he put them up for sale on some street corner.

Mitch, on the other hand, chomped down on the carrot in full view of his mom.

"You don't eat enough," Nancy said.

"I do," he countered. "But I'm betting while I'm here, you're going to do your best to fatten me up."

In the two days he'd been home again, this was the first chance they'd had to talk alone, and he instinctively knew the direction she would take any private conversation between them.

With a long oak table large enough to fit the family, the kitchen didn't offer much room to hide. With his four younger brothers and sisters living at home, there wasn't much privacy in the entire house. And with the way he had been feeling lately, he'd rather have solitary confinement.

"Your father mentioned he'll try to be home early tonight for a change," Nancy said. "But you know how hard it is to get him away from the office. About as difficult as it is to get you back here for a visit."

His mom hadn't intended it, he knew, but her gentle nudging only reminded him he shouldn't be here now. It wasn't that he didn't love his family. He just didn't enjoy coming back to his hometown. And this time, he didn't want to think about the circumstances that had brought about his return. The disaster that had left him lying on a cold concrete floor next to his partner's body.

"I hope you won't have to rush off too soon."

He had missed Thanksgiving by just a few days, and already both she and his dad had hinted they hoped he'd stick around for Christmas. He hadn't had the heart to disillusion them. Hell, he didn't have a reason. Yet.

This enforced time away from the job could end in an instant. Before the holidays, he had appointments scheduled with both the surgeon who had patched up his knee and the department shrink who thought his mind needed some patching, too. Good reports from them would put him right back where he belonged.

Bending down, he kissed her temple. "Let's not get into my visits again right now, Mom, okay?"

"Your lack of visits, you mean." She shot him a glance from eyes the same shade of blue he'd inherited from her. Since he'd gotten his height from his dad, she had to reach up to rest her hand on his shoulder. "I'm worried about you, sweetheart. We're *all* worried about you."

"Don't be." Unable to handle seeing her tears, he turned to grab a stalk of celery he had no taste for. "I'll be fine in no time, just as soon as the last of the stitches dissolve."

Yeah, he'd be all fixed up and ready to get back to work.

Nancy returned to chopping vegetables. "You had a call while you were out to SugarPie's for coffee."

He tensed. "From the department?"

She shook her head. "No, from Jed Garland. He heard you were back in town and wants you to get in touch."

He nodded. As with most of the guys from his high school, he had once worked as a wrangler on Garland Ranch. He hadn't seen his old boss for a while...the same length of time he'd been away from his family. The look in Nancy's eyes said she'd just had a similar thought. That, and knowing why he'd returned now, added fresh layers of guilt.

"I'm surprised it took him this long to find out I'm back in town," he said. "He's usually right on top of everything that happens in Cowboy Creek. A regular old gossip, that's Jed."

To his relief, his mother laughed. "Gossip and more. He's in the matchmaking business now."

*"What?"*

"They've restored the Hitching Post's banquet hall and reopened the honeymoon cabins. Tina and Cole were married from the chapel in June. They're planning to hold the first guest wedding there around Christmas."

"Jed, a matchmaker," he said with a laugh. "Who'd have believed it? Then again, he's always had a knack with people." His former boss had always been there for him, too, especially in those days right out of school when Mitch felt he couldn't talk to his dad. "I should stop by and check in with him."

"You certainly should. He's eager to see you." She set the vegetable platter in the refrigerator. "And when I saw Paz at the L-G Store yesterday, I promised her some of the surplus I'd canned from my garden last fall. Just give me a few minutes to box up a few jars, and you can take them along with you."

Fighting yet more guilt about his need for space from his family, he nodded. He knew how much they all loved him, but he had to have a break from seeing them tiptoeing through the house and talking in hushed voices, as if they were attending a wake.

Yet why wouldn't they act that way in his company?

Thanks to him, a damned good cop was dead.

LATER THAT AFTERNOON, a warm one even for the tail end of November in New Mexico, Mitch parked near the barn on Garland Ranch. He found Jed Garland standing in the sunshine near the corral. As he loped across the yard toward his former boss, Jed smiled.

Since he'd last seen him, the other man's face had developed a few more wrinkles, and his hair had turned completely white. But he still had the same piercing blue eyes and the firmest handshake around.

"Good to see you again, boy." Jed's fingers kept his trapped for another long beat before he let go.

Mitch nodded. "You're looking good yourself. So is the Hitching Post. I see you've made some changes around here."

"Yep. Got the signpost redone and the whole place painted."

"Yeah, my mom said you're in the wedding business again."

"That we are." Jed's guileless expression put Mitch on alert. "We'll be all set whenever you're ready for our services."

"For a wedding?" Laughing, he shook his head. "Thanks, but I'm not the type to settle down."

"That's not what you once said about staying in Cowboy Creek, though, is it? You'd always planned to follow in your dad and granddad's footsteps and join the sheriff's department—yet you went and became a big-city policeman."

"Yeah. I'm a big-time LA cop." Mitch said the words with a hint of bitterness backed by the knowledge of how drastically his plans had changed.

Jed nodded as if he'd read his mind, something he'd always been good at. Mitch found the trait much more disconcerting right this minute than he ever had years ago.

Probably because now he had things to hide.

"With your family's connection to the sheriff's department, I reckon it was a given you'd get involved in law enforcement even after you left town."

He nodded. "Upholding the family tradition." As he'd always known he would.

"Yep. Much as you liked horses and ranching, you never had a doubt about what you wanted to do."

"No." He still hadn't, but his decision now had repercussions he couldn't bring himself to confess to his parents or Jed. His long-held certainty, his downright arrogance that he could handle anything, had let him down when he'd needed it most. Clamping his jaws together, he hooked his biker boot on the lowest fence rung and stared across the corral.

"Let me say, son, I'm sorry about your troubles." Jed's clap on his shoulder hadn't lost any of its strength, either. "I can understand if you're finding your recuperation painful in more ways than one."

His vocal cords seized up, overpowered by the lump in his throat. Looked as though his former boss was still here for him.

Jed Garland was one mighty smart man, but he couldn't know about *all* his doubts. No one could.

Jed rested his forearms on the fence and linked his fingers together. "I'm sure you realize a man doesn't reach success without some failure along the way."

"Yeah," he said harshly, "but *my* failure resulted in someone dying."

"And in your line of work, you think that makes you stand out from the crowd?"

He shot a glance toward the other man. "You've been talking to my dad."

"'Course I have." Jed sighed. "I'm not saying what happened wasn't a tragedy. I'm not saying it's something you can ever shake off. But you're too good a cop—too good a man—not to get past this."

Looking away again, Mitch gripped the rail and squinted into the lowering sun. The bright light made his eyes water.

"Meanwhile," Jed said, "it's good you've come home."

"Temporarily." He hoped he sounded convincing. He lived and breathed law enforcement, had done ever since he was a kid watching his dad and grandpa pinning their badges to their uniforms. There was nothing else he wanted to do with his life. Nothing else he could do.

"You'll have to hang around till Pete and Cole get in from the northern pastures. And Paz will have my hide if I don't get you to stop in to see her. While you're here, you can say hello to the girls."

"The girls?" He gripped the rail even harder.

"Yeah. Tina started off handling the contractors for the upgrades to the Hitching Post, but Jane's been helping out since she moved in a few months ago. And now we've got a wedding booked, Andi's here to pitch in, too."

Jed's three granddaughters.

Tina had grown up on the ranch and become the bookkeeper for the hotel. Jane was a well-respected photojournalist, originally based in New York. And Andi...

Andi was the reason he'd left Cowboy Creek.

"IF I HAVE to look at one more fabric swatch today, I may scream."

At her cousin's pronouncement, Andi Price forced a laugh.

The hotel and its dude ranch activities had always been a big draw for the guests, but their grandfather had recently decided to reopen the banquet hall with a focus on catering wedding receptions.

So far, the one wedding they had scheduled a few months earlier had been canceled, and the business was getting off to a slow start.

"What have *you* got to scream about?" she said to Jane, only half teasing. "I'm the one dealing with the bride-to-be."

"Otherwise known as Bridezilla. Sorry, cuz."

"Don't be." She sighed. "It's the truth. I should have known better than to agree to cater a wedding for the friend of a woman I barely know."

"Yeah. Especially one who wants everything wrapped up in a bow—within a month."

"I thought I was helping Grandpa and you and Tina."

"You are. In Grandpa's words, he's tickled we've got another wedding booked."

"I know." And she couldn't let him down.

The wedding receptions had always been their late grandmother's passion. They all knew Jed was determined to see that part of the business flourish again. As Jane had once said, it only made sense to capitalize on a hotel called the Hitching Post.

"Good thing Tina's around to help," Andi said. "But what would we both do without you?" Jane's career as a photojournalist gave her a good eye for envisioning just about anything. "You know you're the one with the talent for color and line."

"You're not doing badly with those yourself. And the designs you've come up with for the banquet hall are pure genius."

"Thanks. I've attended a lot of receptions and formal dinners since I got married." Thoughts of all the events she had attended once she'd become part of the affluent Price family now blended with other memories she tried not to dwell on. "Knowledge of fancy napkin folds comes with the territory," she attempted to say lightly.

"You're doing a lot more than arranging napkins." Jane tossed a sample book onto the pile with all the others. "But, though I hate to say this, there's an area where you're not doing such a great job."

"Really?" She frowned and looked at everything they had spread out on the tabletop. "What's that?"

"I wish I knew." Jane shook her head. "You've changed since you were here at the end of the summer. There's something bothering you. Don't ask me what, because I have no idea, but I think you ought to let me in on it. We didn't spend all those vacations and holidays together here for nothing, you know."

While their grandfather and cousin had always lived in Cowboy Creek, Jane and Andi had met up at the family ranch only on school breaks. Neither of them had ever stayed at Garland Ranch longer than a summer vacation—until now. Jane had returned only a few months ago to live here permanently.

Andi had come back to help get the new venture off the ground with this Christmas wedding—and for other reasons she tried to shove aside with her bittersweet memories. "Nothing's wrong. I just…felt the kids and I needed a change of scenery. When Grandpa asked me to handle this wedding while you and Tina focused on the business end of things, it seemed like the perfect time for a visit."

Jane's gray eyes narrowed. "Sorry, but I'm not buying that. It might be hard to handle the heat in Fountain Hills, Arizona, but the scenery there is even better than it is here."

"I don't live in Fountain Hills anymore," she said quietly.

"Oh. When you'd told me the other day you and the kids had moved to an apartment, you didn't mention it was in another town." Jane touched her wrist. "Andi, if there's anything I can do, any way I can give you a hand with something, just say the word. I've got some savings built up. I know Grandpa and my dad would help you out in a heartbeat. You know that, too. And wouldn't your mother-in-law be willing to pitch in?"

"It's not money."

Truthfully, it *was* money that worried her—not enough money and not enough life insurance to pay the mortgage. Grant had insisted they could afford the too-big house in their upscale area not far from his mother. With his salary included, they had gotten by. Without it, she had been forced to sell the home where both her children had lived since they'd been born. But she couldn't tell her mother-in-law Grant hadn't provided for his family.

Just as she couldn't reveal to anyone what Grant's real job had been. How did you explain to a man's family that he worked undercover for the CIA?

But now she could tell Jane the truth. Or part of it. "It's not money so much as the need to get some space from Grant's family."

"Things have gotten that bad between you?"

"No." Andi's eyes misted. "They're great." They just didn't know he had told them the same cover story she had told her family, that he worked for a computer company with customers and suppliers all over the world. "Ginnie's always been a fabulous mother-in-law, and everyone else in his family is wonderful. Except...he's been gone for over a year, and they all act as if he's just away on business and will walk in the door again any day now."

She glanced at Jane again. "I loved Grant, you know that. *They* know that. But I've managed to accept that he's gone. I've had to, for Trey and Missy." Her children had given her the strength she'd needed to survive her loss, and now she needed to stay strong for them. "Ginnie and the rest of Grant's family still haven't come to terms with his death. They need—*I* need—to let go and move on. I know that sounds awful—"

"Not awful at all. It's a sad fact of life."

"It's beyond sad. But I just can't keep living in the past. For the kids' sake, I have to think about what comes next." Her two-year-old son and infant daughter were too young to really feel the loss of their daddy, especially when Grant's work assignments often had him out of touch for a month or two at a time. But as they got older, they would realize their loss. It was her responsibility to make sure they never lacked for anything else.

So far, she was doing a poor job.

"Then it's good you're here," Jane said. "You've got the break from Grant's family, and you can plan for the future."

She nodded. Still, despite how determined she might have sounded to Jane, she worried. Her sales assistant job at a clothing store barely covered the rent on her new apartment. She'd had to take the position. With only a year of college behind her, she had left school to get married. Relocating to Arizona, planning a wedding, buying a house and getting swept up in the Price family's social whirl had made her put school off for a while.

After she had gotten pregnant, she had tabled the idea of school indefinitely. Then she had gotten pregnant again…and Grant had died.

The end result was, she had no employable skills to speak of. The only bright spot was having a best friend with a night job who had volunteered to watch the kids while she worked during the day.

The sound of raised voices came from the hotel lobby. Andi jumped to change the subject. "That's Grandpa, and he sounds excited."

They heard a woman's laugh.

"And that's Tina," Jane said. "I wonder what's going on."

They didn't have to wait long to find out. Their cousin Tina entered the dining room. Smiling, she said, "You'll never guess who Grandpa's bringing along here with him."

She was right, at least as far as Andi was concerned.

When Jed Garland walked into the room accompanied by a tall, broad-shouldered man with a noticeable limp, her heart skipped a few critical beats. The man locked gazes with her, and her heart leaped. Never in a million years would she have forgotten those deep blue eyes or that crooked grin or the thick black hair worn just bad-boy long. Never in a million centuries would she have expected—or wished—to run into Mitch Weston again.

She could only hope that since they had last seen each other, he had forgotten all about her.

Or had learned the value of forgiveness.

## Chapter Two

All through the conversation in the dining room, Mitch managed to keep his smile in place. He hadn't wanted to come in here and see Jed's granddaughters, but the man had insisted.

No. Truth was, he hadn't wanted to see Andi again.

Thankfully, his undercover work had prepared him well for slipping into different roles. He'd never had more of a need to hide his true self than he did now. His first glance at blonde, beautiful Andi today had rocked him just the way she had years ago.

Also thankfully, he'd heeded the surgeon's caution to wear his knee brace. Otherwise, he'd swear his legs would have gone out right from under him.

"How long will you be around?" Jed asked.

Instinctively, he knew the man meant how long would he be in Cowboy Creek, a topic he didn't want to get into. He forced a grin and pretended to misunderstand. "Surely you're not inviting me for supper without clearing it with Paz first."

"Of course you'll join us."

He shook his head. "You think you have to worry about Paz skinning your hide? If I didn't show up at home tonight, my mom would have me stuffed and mounted. It's the first time the whole family's sitting down together for a meal since I've gotten back." He shrugged. "Well, it'll be the whole family if my dad manages to make it home."

"He's a good one for sticking to duties," Jed said.

"And," Tina put in, "the day he retires, Cowboy Creek will lose a good sheriff."

"Which probably won't be any time soon." Mitch laughed, happy he'd detoured around the conversational land mine. "Like my grandpa, he always said he would never take off the badge." And like his dad, he wouldn't be keen on retiring, either. He didn't like even being away from the job this long. "Well, I need to head back to town."

"Don't forget that box you said your mama sent along," Jed reminded him.

"Yeah, her garden tomatoes. I'll get them out of the truck now." He moved slowly, giving his healing knee a chance to loosen up, rather than let them all see him hobbling from the room like an old man.

"I can go out with you," Tina volunteered.

"Hold on," Jed said. "I need to talk to you and Jane for a bit." He turned to Andi. "Why don't you go along with Mitch and retrieve that box for Paz? She's eager to see what she can use from it for supper."

Andi nodded. As they left the room, he caught her profile from the corner of his eye. When he and Jed had walked into the dining room, before she'd had time to raise her defenses, he'd seen the sparkle in her blue eyes and the smile on those full pink lips he'd always remembered.

Now, with her gaze frozen and her mouth pressed into a flat, determined line, she looked as if he were marching her to face a firing squad.

She didn't have that far wrong. He planned to fire a

few shots at her. Verbal ones. Questions he'd spent years asking himself.

And he didn't intend to let her go free until he got the answers.

"ALL RIGHT, ABUELO, let's hear it."

Jed frowned. The sound of Mitch's and Andi's footsteps had barely faded from the dining room.

His youngest granddaughter, Tina, sat back in her chair and stared him down. "What's so important I couldn't take a few minutes to give Mitch a hand?"

"I wanted to go over some of those estimates for the last of the cabins again."

Jane laughed. "You're in trouble if you want me here for anything involving numbers. Didn't you always say I'm the artistic one in the family?"

Tina shook her head. "It's not that, Jane. Grandpa's up to his tricks again. I know the signs. So should you." The smile that tugged at her lips gave the lie to her stern expression. "Isn't that right, Abuelo?"

He shrugged. "Yeah, I pulled a few tricks on you both. But I don't hear either of you complaining."

"We aren't," Jane said. "In fact, you know we're glad you're two for two in the matchmaking stakes."

He beamed at her.

"We're very glad," Tina agreed. "Andi's a different story. We all want to see her happy again. But trying to match her up with someone she barely knows may not be the best idea. At least, not right now."

"Huh-uh, cuz," Jane said, "as Grandpa would say, you haven't come close to hitting the mark there. You didn't hang out much with us when Andi and I used to visit. But one summer, I spent plenty of time at the barn because that's where she chose to go. And trust me, it wasn't all due to her love of riding horses."

*"Really?"* Tina's gaze flew from Jane to him and back again.

Barely able to believe this unexpected good fortune, he grinned. Maybe this wouldn't be his toughest match, after all. "You're saying Andi had a hankering for Mitch?"

"I am," Jane confirmed. "A major crush."

"Really," Tina said, thoughtfully this time. "And you think…"

"Yes, I think. Big-time."

"I think, too." But he wasn't yet ready to share the rest of his thoughts on the matter. "And I do more than just let an idea sit in my head. I plan."

"And you scheme," Tina said.

"Yes," Jane said, "and you force people into situations where they can't avoid each other."

"Darn straight, I do. Why wouldn't I? If I didn't, we'd all still be waiting for the two of you to get together with Cole and Pete."

Jane laughed. "So now you're determined to have a try at Andi and Mitch?"

"Darn straight," he repeated.

"Well, you won't get any argument from me, Grandpa. I go along with that."

They both turned to look at Tina.

Quiet, levelheaded, by-the-books accountant Tina looked back at them, meeting their gazes with a frown. "You really think we ought to be pushing Andi into something like this?"

"Not pushing," he said. "Assisting. If there's still interest there, why shouldn't we add a spark to it?"

"Like Grandpa did with you," Jane said softly.

His granddaughters exchanged a glance.

Finally, Tina smiled. "Well, I can't argue with that. All right. You can count me in, too."

"That's my girls," he said.

MITCH AND ANDI left the hotel through the lobby and went down the porch steps, and still, as she walked along beside him, Andi said nothing.

Apprehension showed in the tiny lines around her eyes. Why wouldn't she feel uneasy? She knew as well as he did they had unfinished business to discuss.

He remembered another day they had spent together when she hadn't said a word. When they strolled down to the creek hand in hand, accompanied only by the sounds of crickets chirping. When his heart had thumped so hard he worried she could hear that, too.

Now his heart revved only in anger. Jaw clamped tight, he strode toward the parking area behind the hotel as quickly and steadily as his leg would allow.

"Been a long time," he said as mildly as he could. A half-dozen years had passed since he'd last seen Andi. "I hear a lot has happened in your life."

She nodded. "I'm a mom now, with two children, a boy and a girl."

Her voice sounded strained, yet he couldn't mistake the pride in it. He didn't want to acknowledge even to himself how her statement made his anger rise.

When they were teens, he hadn't thought too far into the future. He had simply known he would be settled down in Cowboy Creek and wearing a gold sheriff's badge. He had also somehow known he would one day be the father of her kids.

Wrong, yet again.

He noticed she hadn't mentioned her husband. In letters, his mom filled him in on all the happenings in

Cowboy Creek. No one knew about his relationship with Andi, but as he had worked with Jed, Nancy put special emphasis on everything concerning Garland Ranch. She had told him about Andi's becoming a widow, losing her husband when he was killed in a car accident while traveling for his job.

"I was sorry to hear what happened," he said.

"Thanks."

She crossed her arms as if the sun had gone behind a cloud and left her chilled. Or as if she needed a comforting hug. He swallowed hard, feeling a small part of his anger slip away. Somehow, he managed to keep from wrapping his arms around her.

He could see the effect the loss had on her. While she was still as beautiful as ever, her face now looked stretched taut. Grief left her with nothing to soften her cheekbones or to fill the hollows beneath them.

Her eyes held a deep sadness. Tiny lines creased the skin in the outside corners. Those lines made him want to touch her. To stroke away her tension.

Instead, he reached into the truck for the box Nancy had sent along with him for the Hitching Post. The action gave him something else to do with his hands. It gave him time to pull himself together. Maybe, if he tried hard enough, that beat of time would let him swallow his remaining anger. For now.

He balanced the box on the truck's hood and turned back to her. "I'm glad Jed sent you out here. It keeps me from having to track you down."

He could see her nerves take hold in the way she brushed her hair away from her temple. The movement distracted him, again making him want to reach out to her. Unfortunately, the urge wasn't strong enough to derail his thoughts for long.

He had all the sympathy in the world for her...but that still couldn't give him answers. "What happened that summer, Andi? You were here one day and gone the next, and that was it. No note, no letter, nothing."

She didn't respond.

"You owe me an explanation, at least," he said harshly. "You walked away from me as if I'd never existed. I thought we had something good going." *Something good?* Hell of an understatement. "I guess, no matter what you'd said then, *thought* is the key word here."

Over near the corral, a horse neighed and one ranch hand called out to another. Andi's silence went on long enough to make him wonder if she would ever answer. But he'd had plenty of practice at holding on, waiting for a witness to make a statement or a perp to make a confession.

Which would she do?

"My mom got sick," she said finally.

"And when she got better, you couldn't get in touch?"

"She didn't get better. She had breast cancer, and she wasn't a survivor. Grandpa didn't tell you?"

He sucked in a breath. "I'd heard from my mom...after your mom passed away. But I didn't know she'd gotten sick back then. Or that it was why you'd left."

"She wouldn't let us tell anyone here, because she didn't want Grandpa to worry."

"Jed didn't know?"

"Not right away. And once Mom got sicker, she didn't want anyone around her except my dad and me. She held out for a long time, and we were grateful for every minute we had left with her. That's why I didn't come back here to visit until...until after she was gone."

Now he couldn't keep from touching her. He rested his hand on her arm, feeling the warmth of her skin and the way her muscle tightened beneath his fingers. "I'm sorry."

She nodded, then grabbed the carton from the hood and rushed away, but not quickly enough to keep him from seeing the tears in her eyes.

He'd gotten answers to his questions, discovered his anger had slipped away, but didn't know what he could find to replace it.

He curled his fingers, trying to hang on to the warmth he would swear he still felt from her skin.

HER ARMS TREMBLING, Andi carried the carton Mitch had given her into the Hitching Post's kitchen. She wasn't shaky from the weight of the box but from seeing him again. And she wasn't ready to consider what had brought on the reaction.

As Andi set the carton down, Paz crossed the room to investigate. "Ah, very nice," she murmured with a born chef's appreciation.

Jane merely leaned forward from her seat at the table to peer into the box. "All those healthy vegetables. They look heavy. I'm surprised Mitch didn't volunteer to carry the box for you."

Andi heard the teasing in her cousin's tone, but couldn't summon the energy to match it. She said simply, "He had to get home."

She wasn't about to tell anyone how abruptly she had turned and walked away. At the porch, she had risked a look over her shoulder and saw him climbing into his truck. Seeing the way he eased into position told her how much he must have been hurting.

She didn't want to think of him in pain.

She didn't want to think of him at all.

"That's good, right, Andi?" Jane said loudly.

She started. "What?"

Paz smiled at her. "I said, tomorrow, I will make my vegetable soup."

"That's great. Sorry, I was daydreaming…" Andi looked toward the door. "I need to check on the kids."

"They're fine," Jane said. "Grandpa has them all in the sitting room."

"Then that's where I'm headed."

"I'll go with you. Unless you need some help, Paz? And if you do, I volunteer Andi." Jane laughed.

"Oh, no, you don't," Paz said, attempting to sound stern. "Pete loves my spicy vegetable soup, and this is your chance to learn how to make it."

At the look on her cousin's face, Andi laughed.

Smiling, she left the two women and went down the hall leading from the kitchen to the hotel's lobby. She could hear voices coming from the sitting room.

Her son gave a high-pitched screech of uncontained laughter. At the sound, tears welled in her eyes. Back home again after their last visit to Cowboy Creek, Trey had reverted to being quiet and withdrawn. The change in him had started not long after Grant's death, and it broke her heart to think that maybe he, like Jane, had sensed changes in her she had hoped no one could see. She hadn't been able to hide her stress, and all her worries kept her distracted. That had to stop, especially if it was already affecting her children.

Coming back to the ranch for the holidays and to oversee the wedding had been the right decision. Being with Tina's son, Robbie, and Pete's kids was good for Trey.

But being around Mitch wasn't good for *her*.

Thank goodness he had turned down Jed's invitation to join them for dinner. Before that, she had noticed how quickly he deflected the question about him staying. She was certain he knew as well as she did Grandpa had meant his visit to Cowboy Creek.

In any case, his answer might not have mattered. He had a long drive between his parents' house in town and Garland Ranch. Judging by the trouble he'd had climbing into his truck, today's trip to the hotel could very well be his last while he was here.

In the sitting room, she found Jed in his favorite chair, holding Missy on his lap. "You'll be spoiling her, Grandpa," she scolded gently.

"Then she'll be spoiled," he said with a grin. "I'm taking every chance I can get to hold her. She's been away too long. You all have."

As she took a seat on one of the chairs near them, she forced a smile. Jed hadn't made any secret of the fact that he wanted her and the kids to move to the ranch permanently.

She wanted only to prove she could take care of her family on her own.

Trey crossed the room to them, thumping his chest with one hand. "Look, Mommy. Look what I got."

Rachel, Pete's five-year-old, followed in his footsteps. "It's Robbie's badge. Robbie let me play with it and I shared it with Trey."

"That's very nice of you, Rachel. And that's a very nice badge, sweetheart." She tapped the plastic star-shaped pin and touched her son's cheek.

"I'm the chef."

"You mean sheriff," Rachel corrected. She turned to Andi. "He means sheriff. Grandpa Jed said Mitch has a badge, too. Didn't you, Grandpa Jed?"

"I sure did."

Yes, Mitch had a badge. And a gun and an injury and a dangerous job. Grant's position had the potential for danger, too. They'd both known it. But Mitch's could expose him to risk every day of his life.

"Mitch is going to show me his badge," Rachel announced.

"Well," Andi said, "I think he must have forgotten. He's gone home already."

"But he's coming back tomorrow."

She froze. The clock on the wall chimed, saving her from having to reply for a moment. When it stopped, she looked from Rachel to Jed. "Mitch is coming here tomorrow?"

"Yeah," Robbie put in. "Grandpa says so."

Nodding, Jed patted the phone on the end table beside his chair. "Just spoke to Nancy, and she confirmed he's got nothing on his schedule. I told her I want him to come by and talk with me for a bit. And I want to make sure he catches up with Pete."

She fisted her hands in her lap. She didn't want to see Mitch again.

Watching him in the dining room surrounded by her family had been bad enough. It allowed her too much time to resurrect the many sweet memories she had buried long ago.

But to her dismay, standing outside with him had been so much worse. Being with him had forced her to see what she didn't want to admit.

Time and distance and even marriage to a man she loved with all her heart hadn't destroyed her feelings for Mitch.

## Chapter Three

"Did living in LA turn you off your mom's good cooking?"

At his dad's question, Mitch started. He looked up to find everyone at the table sitting with their eyes trained on him. The combined stares of his parents, two brothers and two sisters added up to way more attention than he needed.

"Are you kidding?" He forked up a chunk of onion, chewed and swallowed it. "I'm just trying to draw out the pleasure. You always did tell me I ate too fast."

"You both do that," Nancy said.

"Hazard of the profession," his dad agreed.

Mitch nodded and tried to ignore the elephant in the room. Since he'd been home, he'd had plenty of hugs and kisses from the girls and lots of slaps on the back from the boys. He couldn't deny his family's happiness at having him here again. He just hated to see them all suffering on his behalf.

Everybody wanted to comfort him for his loss, he knew, but no one wanted to be the first to bring it up. His dad insisted on acting as though nothing much had happened. Even his mom hadn't cornered him yet, as he'd expected.

And he didn't want to think about recent events at all.

He glanced down at his plate. The roast Nancy had made for supper, always his favorite, tasted dry as dust. It wasn't Mom's good cooking that had him distracted, though. It was the vision of a slim woman with long blond hair and sad eyes.

"Your mom said you were out to Jed's place this afternoon." His dad passed him the meat platter. "How's everything at Garland Ranch?"

"And how's Daffodil?" his younger sister Laurie asked. Daffodil was an old mare living out her days at the ranch.

"I didn't go near the corral," he had to confess.

Like the typical teen she was, Laurie rolled her eyes. She loved anything that walked on four legs, but especially horses.

"You need to drop by the office," his dad said, "and say hello to the boys."

He nodded. He knew most of the men in Cowboy Creek's sheriff's department. Heck, he'd grown up with them. Considering what had happened, seeing them didn't rank high on his list. Then again, stopping by the office gave him something to do.

It might help keep his mind off Andi and his decision not to visit the ranch again.

"Oh, Mitch," Nancy said. "I forgot to tell you. You hadn't made it home yet when Jed called. He wants you to go back out to the ranch tomorrow. He seems to have something important on his mind."

Again, he had to appreciate the work that had trained him to keep his reactions hidden. He also suddenly found a lot more to like in his dad's idea. "Thanks for passing the message along. I'll probably be a while at the department tomorrow. But I'll get out there again one of these days." On another trip back home. When Andi wasn't there.

"From what your mom says, maybe you ought to make the trip a priority," his dad suggested.

"I can go with you after school," Laurie offered. "I can see Daffodil and then go for a ride."

"And," his mother said, "I told Jed I'd send along some more vegetables for Paz."

His brothers volunteered to help her box up the canning jars.

As he considered the conversation, Mitch sat back in his chair and shifted his leg to make himself more comfortable.

Nothing had been mentioned about what had brought him home. No furtive looks had been exchanged between anyone at the table. Yet somehow, he felt certain every member of his family had given the elephant in the room a strong, steady push in the right direction.

At least, from their perspective.

LATE THE NEXT AFTERNOON, accompanied by nonstop chatter from Laurie, Mitch drove up the road to Garland Ranch for the second time in two days.

She went on about her classes and friends and riding and the holiday open house Jed held every year at the hotel. He hadn't made it back for one of those parties since he'd left town to go to school. Maybe he'd be gone for this one.

He thought again about his family ganging up on him over today's trip. *Something* had made them all suddenly think the return to Garland Ranch would do him good.

Sure, they wanted him to relax and unwind and go back to being the son and brother they'd always known. That wasn't going to happen, no matter how much they tried. He would never be the man he was before the incident. The incident…

He'd trained himself to use that cop-speak every time he thought about the day. To put a professional spin on an event leaving more than one man dead. To keep from obsessing over the knowledge his partner's death was personal and a memory he would always carry with him.

He ran his hand over his face, then opened the window all the way, hoping the fresh air would chase away the images filling his mind.

"Hey," Laurie yelped. "It's December. You want me to catch pneumonia and miss the party?"

"You'd go to that open house if you had both legs and one arm in a cast."

"Sure would." She laughed.

He thought again of his family's efforts to get him out to the ranch. Their methods had sent up a red flag. Something wasn't right about their determination.

"You do much riding out at Jed's?" he asked.

"Not as much anymore," she admitted.

"Mom says you spend weekends there, though."

To his surprise, her cheeks turned red. "Well, I go to see Daffodil. She's old, you know."

"Yeah. She had been getting up there even when I worked the ranch. She always thought she should be treated like a queen."

"Jed said she earned that right. And Eddie… I mean, Pete thinks she likes when I visit."

"Sounds like Eddie-I-mean-Pete knows a thing or two about horses."

Laughing, she smacked his arm, the way she had done a hundred times before. It surprised him to realize he'd missed that, along with roughhousing with the boys.

"All right," she said, "I meant Eddie. He takes care of the stables."

Just the job he'd had the first time he'd seen Andi. The luckiest day of his life till then.

It looked as though his little sister might have the same kind of good fortune. Maybe hers would last. "Am I going to have to play biggest brother and give the guy a warning about being good to my sister?"

"Show him your gun. That'll work even better."

His hands clamped onto the steering wheel so tightly, he could barely make the turn into the drive. The flash of memory that hit made him wince.

*PTSD*, the psychiatrist assigned to him after the shooting had labeled it, the body giving way as remembered trauma took control. According to the shrink, the stress showed up in different ways.

Yeah, he'd dealt with that, right after the…incident. It had eased up a lot since then. He was fine. Fine, except for those nights he woke up in a sweat. And those times he paced his apartment to outrun the demons chasing him.

And, so it seemed, when he heard his baby sister joke about his weapon.

He parked near the corral on Garland Ranch and shot a glance at the woman who stood outside the fence, her back to them. Andi. He thought of all the drugs the shrink had offered him and he had refused. Seeing Andi again made him feel better than any drug ever could.

With one boot planted on the lowest rail, she watched a blond-haired little boy on a small Shetland. Her son, Trey, he had no doubt.

"That's him," Laurie said, as if she'd read his mind. But one glance told him *her* mind was on the teenager leading the horse. He'd wager he knew who that was, too.

By the time he had eased out of the truck and made his way around it, Laurie had left him far behind.

Either Andi had no interest in newcomers or she hadn't recognized Laurie as his sister, because she hadn't moved from her spot near the rail. He had time to notice the fall of blond hair around her shoulders and the way her jeans hugged her curves. He even had time to remember how it had felt to hold those curves. By the time she turned to look his way, he'd broken into a sweat brought on by the memories. *That* was the kind of healing meds he needed.

Dragging his shirtsleeve across his brow, he took a deep breath. Then he moved forward, cursing his knee brace and every halting step she had to see.

She clung to the top rail the way he'd gripped the steering wheel. Her gaze shot toward the barn.

"Eddie and Laurie are with the boy. Your son?"

She nodded.

"Tell me about your kids."

The light in her face told him he'd said the right thing. The same light he once saw when she looked at him.

"Trey is two, almost three."

"Ah. The terrible twos?" When her eyes widened in surprise, he shrugged. "I remember my brothers and sisters going through them."

"Well, I'll admit my son has had his moments." A smile lit her face even more. "It's been good for Trey to be here on the ranch and around Tina's son, Robbie, and Pete's two kids. You remember Pete Brannigan?"

He nodded. "Jed said he's ranch manager now. And he did mention the kids."

"Yes. He has a girl and boy of his own. All three of the kids are just old enough not to take any interest yet in my daughter, Missy."

"She's…?"

"Six months."

"Yeah, she's young." He did the math. By rights, he and Andi could have started a family of their own before either of her kids had been born. But she had left him, and they had lost their chance.

The sudden faraway look in her eyes prompted him into speech. "Jed tells me you're staying at the hotel."

"Temporarily," she shot back.

He winced at the echo of his response when Jed had mentioned his coming home. Hopefully, he hadn't sounded as defensive. Looked as if Andi didn't plan to stay around Cowboy Creek. Neither did he.

"I'm only here through the holidays," she added.

"This is just a short visit for me, too."

"And then you'll go back to Los Angeles."

She sounded as if what he did concerned her. He couldn't trust that he'd read her right. But he would bet good money she hadn't forgotten their summer.

He would never forget that day he'd looked across the barn to find the hottest girl he'd ever seen standing in the doorway, a blonde angel in a T-shirt, jeans and riding boots. He'd fallen head over heels and would have sworn she'd done the same.

Every day, once his work at the ranch was done, they had spent as much time together as they could. Until that one day she had just up and left without saying a word.

But here they were.

He had the feeling she was about to repeat history and walk off. "I belong in LA," he said, half to remind himself and half to keep her with him, as pathetic as both of those felt for him to admit. "I'm with the police department."

"That's a dangerous job. A tough one for you, and just as hard on your wife and kids."

As she ought to have seen by her own husband's death,

in the right—or wrong—circumstances, any job had its risks. He shook his head. "I don't have a wife. Or any family there. It's just me."

Alone at home. On his own on the job.

And now standing here beside the girl who'd started him down that road.

He couldn't stop himself from reaching up to gently stroke the fine, lined skin near her eye.

"I'm not wearing well," she said with a forced laugh.

"We've all gotten older." But maybe not wiser. He cupped her cheek with his palm. The warmth spreading through his hand more than made up for the risk he'd taken in touching her. For a brief moment, she tilted her head, resting against his hand. Her reaction closed the gap left by all the years they had lost. It finally chased away all his resentment.

Her eyes misted. She turned away. "I'm sorry about not contacting you. Everything was just too much for me. I had to focus on my mom."

She looked toward the barn, as if planning to head over there. He didn't want her to leave.

"That's a big load for an eighteen-year-old to handle," he said.

"For anyone to handle, believe me." She sighed. "Sometimes, life doesn't seem fair."

"That's because it isn't. We all get the luck of the draw—and sometimes it's bad luck."

Just what he'd heard from everyone back in LA.

After a quick nod, Andi walked away.

He leaned against the rail, easing the pressure on his knee, and watched her go. That summer afternoon years ago, he'd had no idea he wouldn't see her again. Would the same thing happen now? Was he simply destined to have bad luck when it came to her?

Though he could parrot the words his buddies on the force had told him, that didn't mean he wanted to accept their verdict about the situation.

And though everything in him said he should keep his distance from Andi, that didn't mean he had the strength to heed his own warning.

# Chapter Four

As she crossed the yard to the barn, Andi could almost feel Mitch's gaze on her back. She could definitely still feel the warmth filling her from the touch of his hand against her cheek. In that one all-too-brief moment, she had changed into a teen again, and he had become the boy she loved. In his eyes in that moment, she saw the boy who loved her, too.

But their teenagers-in-lust days were long over.

Resolutely, she focused on the group standing in the barn doorway and kept moving toward them, away from Mitch and his warm hands and his crooked smile and his unfamiliar stiff-legged walk.

When she approached the group, her son gave her the wide grin that always reminded her so much of his daddy. "Mommy, I rided Bingo."

"I saw you," she said. "You did a great job."

"He did," Eddie, the stable hand, agreed. "I'll be happy to give him another practice run anytime."

"I'm sure Trey would love that."

"Yeah, Mommy, wanna ride horse. Bi-i-ig horse."

"Don't you worry, mister," Eddie said, "we'll get you up on Bingo again tomorrow. How's that?"

"Yay!" Trey clapped his hands. No sign of the terrible twos now, as Mitch had mentioned.

With a smile, she watched Eddie ruffle her son's hair. She didn't need a policeman's skills to note that the tall, quiet teen grew much more talkative every time Mitch's sister Laurie arrived at the ranch. Whenever she saw the two of them together, the pair made her think of Mitch and herself.

With luck, this couple's summer romance would end more happily than her and Mitch's had done.

When he came to stand beside her, she turned to Trey. "Come on, sweetie, we need to go back to the hotel."

"I don't wanna! Wanna see Daff now."

"So do I," Laurie said quietly over his head. "Is it okay if I take him with me for just a few minutes?"

"I'll go and keep an eye on things," Eddie said.

His tone made it evident he considered himself responsible for everything on the ranch. Just the way Mitch had when she'd met him.

The trio entered the barn.

She went to take a seat on one of the stools the cowhands had left a few yards from the doorway. She hoped Mitch would get the hint, would follow the rest of them in to the stalls or turn and go to the hotel.

But no, he was ambling her way, moving slowly. Maybe to control his limp?

She tried not to stare. Not to let her emotions show in her expression. As a teenager, he had been a star athlete, she knew. Football quarterback. Pitcher for Cowboy Creek's baseball team. Whatever had happened to him on the job, it would devastate him if he couldn't return to being just as active.

He took the stool beside hers, his leg stretched out before him. He sat so close, she could count the stitches running down the leg of his jeans. "Seems like Jed's training up another hand to join the crew."

"Grandpa's good at that."

"Yeah," he agreed. "And I should know."

"You needed to be trained?"

"Sure did. I might have bummed a ride or two on a friend's horse when I was a kid, which meant I could handle myself in the saddle, but that was about it."

"Why did Grandpa take you on in the first place?"

He raised a brow. "This is a dude ranch. Considering all the charm and good looks I had back then, you really have to ask that question?"

Of course, she didn't have to ask. She remembered. He'd had plenty of charm and tons of good looks, and the years hadn't taken any of that away. Not that she would ever admit it to him. "You don't need either of those to groom a horse."

"Ha," he said with a laugh. "You never saw me trying to charm Daffodil on one of her cranky days. But Jed probably thought I'd make a good candidate for working with the hotel guests. Growing up in a family of seven, I learned how to get along with people. Like that kid in there." He jerked his thumb toward the barn doorway. "That one's a real talker."

"When your sister's around."

"Is that so? Well, I seem to remember girls having that effect on me. Especially you." He'd lowered his voice to a husky murmur.

She wrapped her arms around her waist and fought an urge to run.

"Tina was always the quietest cousin," he said, "but you were on the quiet side, too. At first, I couldn't get you to say two words in a row to me. Maybe it's because you were an only child."

No, because she was a tongue-tied teenager who

blushed every time he looked at her. A tendency she didn't seem to have outgrown.

"If not for you wanting to ride," he said, "I'd bet I never would have met you."

If he only knew. On previous vacations here, she had always enjoyed riding. Her interest had skyrocketed the summer she had discovered the new stable hand with the tousled black hair, stripped to the waist of his low-riding jeans, pitching hay into a stall. Suddenly, along with riding, she had felt the urge for twice-daily visits to Daffodil. She had dragged poor Jane, who couldn't have cared less about horses, along with her for company. And camouflage.

"You're still quiet," he said.

She shrugged. "I guess we don't have much to say to each other, do we? We never did much together, except…"

"Except hang out at the barn and sneak away to make out every chance we got?"

Her cheeks burned. "We were kids, Mitch—"

"We're grown-ups now."

"—and that's all in the past. We don't need this trip down memory lane."

"Why not? They're fond memories, aren't they?"

She heard bitterness in his tone but read something else in his face. Something she couldn't afford to see. Instead, she gazed past the corral in the direction of the creek. Another thing she couldn't afford to envision. "Fond memories? Even the final ones?"

From the corner of her eye, she saw his hand clench on his thigh. Why was she reminding him about the way things had ended?

Because she knew they couldn't start anything between them again.

"I'd better go check on Trey."

He laid his hand on her arm. "Maybe I'll give you a second chance for walking away without a word."

"Thanks. But maybe I don't want one." She pulled her arm free.

"I don't need to ask if you still feel something for me, Andi. Your reaction when I touched you a few minutes ago already gave me the answer."

She shook her head. "That was just another quick trip down memory lane."

"Yeah? And don't your memories match mine?" He leaned toward her.

It took more effort than she wanted to look away from him. "Nothing matches anymore, Mitch."

"That sounds like a woman at the end of her rope. What's wrong?"

The question made her jump, but she forced herself to turn to him again. "Nothing's wrong."

"You know, one of the first things they teach rookies is to notice a perp's expression. Always watch the ones who won't look you in the eye—but pay equal attention to the ones who stare you down."

"I told you, nothing's wrong. When I said nothing matches, I just meant we don't have anything in common anymore." She rose from the stool. If he caught her eye again, he would trap her in that lie.

A few hurried steps past him took her into the barn, where she hoped the cool shade would ease the flush in her cheeks. What she would need to cool the rest of her, she didn't know.

Yes, she had lied. She and Mitch had plenty in common. A mutual interest in each other. Leftover lust from their summer together. And somehow, a spark that survived despite the fact she had left him without a word.

Stunned by his close encounter with Andi, Mitch stayed in place on the stool.

He'd been so wrapped up in the idea of seeing her again today, he had spent most of the morning exercising his leg on a slow walk through town, made only a brief trip to the sheriff's office after lunch and found himself sitting outside the school waiting to pick up his sister the minute the final bell rang.

Now he had arrived at the ranch, things hadn't gone nearly the way he'd planned.

A black stallion trotted into the stable yard. Mitch recognized the cowboy astride the horse—Pete Brannigan, his former wrangling buddy and now the manager of Garland Ranch. By the time Pete dismounted, Mitch had risen to his feet.

The other man approached him, leading his mount. "Jed told me you were back in town. Been a heck of a long time, Mitch."

"Yeah, it has."

As they shook hands, Eddie came to lead the horse away. Mitch noted Laurie walking beside the boy. He tried not to notice Andi and her son emerging from the barn. She nodded at Pete before turning away.

The foreman eyed him. "I'm glad you stopped by. If you've got time, how about you give me a chance to shower, then come on over for a brew?" Pete lived in the manager's house on the property, barely the length of a couple of baseball fields from the corral.

"Sure. Jed wanted us to get together. We might as well kick back while you tell me what that's about."

"Not a clue," Pete said. "I saw him around noontime,

but he didn't say a word. You'll have to find out from him for us both. Hey, Andi," he called.

She turned back to face them. Mitch saw how carefully she kept from looking his way. No matter what she said, there was something not right. He'd have to prove that to himself...to make up for the last time he hadn't followed his instincts.

"The boss was looking for this former cowboy earlier. Take Mitch along to the Hitching Post and help him track down Jed, will you?"

When she nodded, Pete strode into the barn.

At a much slower pace, Mitch walked to catch up with Andi and her boy. One look at her brittle smile and suddenly rigid shoulders told him how she felt about having him join them. She couldn't have cared that much about escorting him to the hotel. Maybe she was afraid of giving herself away.

No matter how quickly she'd backed off from him and run into the barn, it had been too late. He'd already seen the truth in her widened eyes and reddening cheeks, just as he had in her reaction to his touch over at the corral. She wanted him just as much as she had years ago. But something was bothering her. Holding her back. Something she didn't want to share with him, and maybe with anyone.

"You cowboy?" her son asked.

The kid must have remembered Pete calling him a former cowboy. He shook his head. "No, I'm a cop."

"What's a cop?"

"A policeman. You know, like a sheriff. With a uniform and a badge."

"A badge? *Mine.*"

Andi took his hand. "You borrowed Robbie's badge, Trey, remember?"

*"Mine,"* the kid repeated.

*Mine,* Mitch had once thought when it came to the kid's mother.

Wishing something so didn't make it happen. He'd first learned that years earlier with Andi's abrupt departure. He'd had his latest lesson only a few weeks ago during an undercover op shot to hell.

Feeling he had failed in both instances didn't sit well with him at all. He couldn't save his partner, but he sure could try to find out what troubled Andi.

"JED IS OUT by the honeymoon cabins, I think," Paz told them. "Tina wanted to show him something the workmen had done."

Sagging in relief, Andi rested one hip against the kitchen table. With her son's short legs, the walk back to the hotel had seemed to last forever. She and Mitch had discovered both the sitting room and Tina's office empty. Now, thanks to Paz, she could send Mitch off on his own.

"Looks like you're busy in here," he said.

Paz nodded. Cooling racks filled with cakes and cookies had taken over almost every flat surface. The kitchen smelled of cinnamon and cloves. "It's never too early to start my Christmas baking."

"Cookie, Paz," Trey demanded.

"What do you say?" Andi prompted him.

"Please."

Smiling, Paz took a cookie from one of the racks.

"Let's go track down Jed," Mitch said.

Andi frowned. "You can do that on your own. I'll stay here with Trey."

"I think I've forgotten how to get to the cabins."

She glanced at him, then away again. After what he had said about cops, she didn't know which was worse from his perspective, locking gazes with him or refusing to look his way at all. She knew what was better for her. Looking. Staring. Getting her fill.

Better for her, but much too risky.

"That's fine, Andi," Paz said. "You leave Trey with me and go right along with Mitch."

"Great," he said, halfway across the room without waiting for her answer.

Grimly, she followed him out to the porch and down the steps. He took his time, favoring his bad leg. Despite her irritation with him, she had to bite her lip to keep from asking how much he hurt.

She was so wrapped up in concern for him, she hadn't realized he'd reached the bottom step. He turned back, catching her off guard. Instinctively, she bit down harder, then winced from her own pain.

"It is that bad?" he asked. "Seeing how I hobble down steps like a two-year-old who's just learned to walk?"

"You handled those steps quite a bit better than my two-year-old does," she said matter-of-factly. Still, knowing how Mitch must feel made her eyes mist.

"Those tears for me?"

"Of course they're not." While she had stopped a couple of steps up, he stood on the ground, putting them at eye level. This time, she was determined not to look away, no matter how his cop's training would interpret her stare. No matter how shaky her reaction to his blue eyes left her feeling. "I accidentally bit my lip and it hurts. Not as much as your knee must, though, I'm sure."

"I don't need your pity, Andi."

"That wasn't pity. It was a not-very-smooth attempt to find out what happened."

"Why? So you can fix it?"

"I never said—"

"You didn't have to. There's nothing wrong with me a few weeks of rest won't cure. And maybe this."

Before she could blink, he had cupped the back of her head as gently as he had cupped her cheek, urging her toward him. Once his mouth met hers, she had nothing but the memories of another time and another place and all the feelings that came with them.

For this one long, heart-stopping, teenager-in-lust-again moment, she loved Mitch Weston as desperately as she had the last day they had been together. She kissed him as desperately, too, without a thought for her tender lip or her obligations or anything but how she'd always felt when Mitch held her. He was broader now, sturdier, more muscled…and an even better kisser.

Reluctantly, she pulled herself together, resting her hands on his wide shoulders to anchor herself. No, to prepare herself. Finally, she pushed away.

Her legs trembling, she went down the rest of the steps, fighting the urge to raise her hand to her mouth. To touch the warmth he had left against her lips. To hold back the words she would not and couldn't afford to say.

With unsteady hands, she smoothed her hair as she attempted to catch her breath. "Are you crazy? It's broad daylight and we're out here in the open and anyone could have seen us. I told you I don't want to fix you." *Liar.* "So just what was *that* supposed to prove?"

"I thought it might help speed the healing."

"Of my lip?"

"No, my knee." His chest rose, as if he were struggling with his breathing, too. He gave her a crooked smile. "All right, that was also to prove you haven't forgotten me any more than I've forgotten you."

"Maybe I haven't. They say you never forget your—"

*first love* "——first kiss. But I've had other kisses since then."

He whistled. "That's cold, Andi."

"That's the truth."

"All of it?"

She stiffened. "What do you mean?"

"C'mon, don't play dumb with me." His laugh sounded strained. "You kissed me back just now."

"Like I had a choice?"

"We always have choices." For a moment, his face hardened and his eyes looked bleak.

"I don't think so. Not always." He was remembering their past. Good. She wouldn't have to lay things out for him. And hopefully, once she had finished here, she would never again have to face a sneak attack on her pitifully weak defenses. "When I left you that summer, it wasn't my decision. But I *am* making the choice to walk away now."

## Chapter Five

So much for the shy little Andi he had once known. The girl he'd had to coax out of her shell had grown into a strong woman whose still-quiet manner hid one heck of a sucker punch. He could use her as the bad cop to his good cop during an interrogation. He could even admire her skill—if not for the fact that she'd used it against him... and then walked away.

He had changed from the day he first met her, too, in more ways than he wanted to deal with at the moment. But despite everything, he still had a few skills of his own, including his bulldog tenacity when it came to getting to the truth of a matter.

He glanced after Andi, whose hip-swaying departure just about wiped her words from his memory bank. It definitely overrode any annoyance he'd felt at getting sucker punched.

Besides, he'd faced a hell of a lot worse and was still standing. He wasn't about to let her knock him down. Or to let her get away.

He followed her across the Hitching Post's backyard toward the cabins a few hundred yards ahead. "Looks like Jed's had the honeymoon havens fixed up, along with the rest of the place."

"Yes," she said shortly, not looking at him. "I'm surprised you noticed the improvements, considering you didn't seem to recall much about the cabins."

He laughed. She had seen through his ruse. No big deal. He'd never hoped to get away with claiming he didn't know the location of the site—not when they'd once spent a rainy afternoon making out in one of those honeymoon havens.

In two strides, he caught up to her. "I recall plenty. But you want to help jog the rest of my memories?" When her cheeks turned pink, making her eyes look even more blue, he couldn't hold back a smug smile. Yeah, she remembered that day, too.

Up ahead, Jed and his granddaughter Tina came around the side of one of the cabins. Jed hailed them with a wave.

They met halfway, in the shade of a few pines that would protect the cabins from the sun of a long New Mexico summer.

"How's everything?" Andi asked Jed.

"Looking just fine."

"The contractors only finished up the remaining cabins this past week," Tina explained.

Mitch nodded. "My mom said you've all done a lot of renovations inside the hotel, too."

"We sure have," Jed said. "You'll have to get Andi to take you on the grand tour."

He sensed more than saw her stiffen beside him.

"Of course," she said too politely. "But right now I've got to get back and take care of business."

"Right," Tina said. "We need to get our order ready for the wedding favors. I'll go back with you."

Again, he felt rather than saw Andi's reaction—relief as she instantly turned away. He went to follow her, then paused, recalling why they had come out this way to begin with. "I got word you wanted me to stop by again," he said to Jed.

The older man nodded. "Yeah. Let's sit. You girls go on ahead. Your old grandpa can't keep up."

"Oh, you—" Andi cut herself off, but Mitch had picked up on her tone. She'd held back a teasing response—because of *him*?

"Okay, Abuelo," Tina said. "See you both later."

As the women left, Jed gestured to a wooden bench on the porch of the nearest cabin.

He nodded. Though he hadn't been on his feet for that long, he felt grateful for the chance to sit again.

No matter what Andi had begun to say about Jed's ability to get around, he had to admit, at the moment, the older man's healthy stride would put his to shame. It wasn't pain that drove him to the bench but the stiffness that locked up his knee from time to time. Sitting was the worst danged thing he could do for it, but he'd rather have the opportunity to get limbered up again before he had to cross the yard with Jed. With luck, he would manage a few stretches stealthily enough to keep his former boss from noticing.

He gave thanks Andi had left. Her denial hadn't carried much weight, not when her eyes had filled with pity, something he refused to accept from anyone and especially not from her.

After they took their seats on the bench, he watched the women cross the yard, Tina's dark, waist-length braid contrasting sharply with Andi's flowing blond waves. No doubt in his mind which sight he preferred. The thought of running his hands through Andi's hair made more than just his bad knee suddenly ache from stiffness. Made him realize how hot he'd gotten over the girl who'd left him behind.

More than anything, his reactions made him see staying close to her might be more of a challenge than he had anticipated.

"Nice view, isn't it?"

Startled, he turned to stare at Jed. He'd forgotten he had company on this bench.

Jed waved his hand. "A pleasant view of the ranch for any honeymooners who stay out here instead of in the hotel."

"Yeah...it's nice scenery." Especially over near the hotel, where the women were climbing the porch steps. "So, you wanted to see me again."

"I do." Jed ran his hand over his pure white hair.

An unmistakable tell. Mom had been right. Something was up with Jed. And the familiar gesture told Mitch his former boss was about to clue him in. "What's up?"

"Your mama says your time is pretty much your own, and I could use your help."

"Anything I can do, you know I will."

Jed smiled. "I figured that. Well, you know we tend to get busy here around the holidays."

"I remember." The dude ranch had always been popular with folks wanting a break from colder climates.

"Now we've got Christmas *and* a wedding to prepare for, both coming up in less than a month. My girls are doing most of the work on their own, and they could use an extra pair of hands."

Mitch nodded slowly.

"Normally, I'd get a couple of the boys in here to give them some assistance. But we're shorthanded, and Pete's up to his eyeballs in work as it is. If you could manage to spend some time around here, you'd be doing us all a favor."

Mitch nodded again. Compared to some of Jed's plans,

this one sounded harmless. And he had meant it when he said he would do anything to help Jed.

To tell the truth, he would be doing himself a few favors, too.

He could avoid his family's hushed voices and averted gazes.

He could bypass some trips to the sheriff's department in town. No matter how often his dad encouraged him to drop in, he knew how all those visits would make him look. He'd seem no better than an old retired cop who took his vacations anywhere from Maine to Alaska but spent those days hanging out with the local law.

Most of all…best of all…he would have a reason to hang around the ranch. A chance to be near Andi and to find out what was up with her.

If she wouldn't tell her family what was worrying her, she'd have to tell someone. She needed *an outlet*, as his department-assigned shrink would say. Considering her decision to walk away from him, getting her alone had presented a problem. Jed had just handed him the solution.

With all those perks attached to the request, how could he turn the man down?

He couldn't appear too eager, though. "Sure," he said casually. "I'll be happy to lend a hand. For whatever time I'm in town."

"WHAT DO YOU think of this design?" Andi turned the pattern book on Tina's desk to show her cousins the photo she was indicating.

With the waitress on duty ready to set the tables for dinner, they'd had to move all their samples from the dining room into Tina's small office off the lobby. It didn't matter to her where they worked, as long as she kept busy enough to keep her mind off Mitch…and that kiss that had made her lose control.

Her face burning, she glanced quickly at her cousins. Luckily, Jane and Tina had both switched their attention to the pattern book.

Jane looked at the fabric swatch in the photo. "I like the other one better."

"I like this one. Then Tina gets to choose."

"Oh, no, I don't," their cousin said. "You two are the experts."

"We need a tiebreaker."

"And if Tina doesn't want to be on the spot," Jane said, "she shouldn't be. Shay's in the kitchen. Don't you think we should get her in on this? She's got a good eye, too."

"Great idea," Tina said.

Shay, who was a frequent visitor to the Hitching Post, was dropping off an order of ice cream. Though Paz made the desserts for the hotel dining room, they had contracted SugarPie's to provide the wedding cakes and pastries for the receptions. But when it came to ice cream, they relied on the Big Dipper, the shop not far from SugarPie's in the heart of Cowboy Creek's small business district.

As Tina left the office to track down the other woman, Andi caught Jane looking at her with a thoughtful expression.

"I see Mitch is back again," Jane said. "And he appeared just when you happened to be at the corral."

She snapped her head up. "That was a coincidence."

"On your part or his?"

"What does that mean?"

"It seems *way* too coincidental he showed up at the same time you were standing there waiting."

"I wasn't *waiting*. I was checking on Trey." She caught Jane's grin and realized her cousin was teasing. She also knew she had overreacted. Forcing a smile, she added, "So…you suspect Eddie and Laurie of synchronizing the clocks on their cell phones?"

"No, actually, that hadn't occurred to me." Jane's tone turned serious again. "Maybe fate stepped in, leading Mitch here just the right time."

"No. It was Grandpa wanting to see him. And Laurie asking him to bring her to the ranch for a ride." Hoping to close the subject, she glanced at the pattern book again. "There's no need to wait for Shay. I don't know why you're digging your heels in over this. Now, look. This morning, you agreed with me this pattern's a better match for the tableware."

"Yeah, and I've always agreed that you and Mitch made a good match."

"*Jane.* Please."

"Now, you look," Jane said quietly. "You can't hide anything from me. I know how you felt that summer you were seeing him. And I heard you crying the night before you left the ranch. You cared a lot. So did he. You two really had a chance together."

A chance she had blown back then, and that circumstances now put out of her reach. "That was a long time ago." Her children's births and husband's death ago.

"And here you are, in town at the same time."

"Just another coincidence."

"I won't argue that. But my point is, how likely is it this will happen again soon?"

Focusing on the pattern book kept her from meeting Jane's eyes. It couldn't help close her ears to Jane's softly spoken words.

"Maybe you both need to take this second chance."

Shay walked into the office, saving Andi from a response.

"Shay," Jane said, "you're still planning to waitress for us the night of the wedding?"

"Oh, yes, I'll be here. I'm looking forward to it."

Still shaken by Jane's statement, Andi fought to focus on the other woman. "How's your gran?" They all knew Shay's elderly grandmother had been having some health issues.

"Not too bad. I'm on my way to pick her up now. But Tina said you wanted to show me something?"

"Yes, if you have a few minutes." She indicated the two samples. "Which one?"

"This one's a better match," Shay said immediately, pointing.

"Perfect," Jane said. "You've got a good eye, too."

Shay had chosen the same pattern Jane had so suddenly been unable to make up her mind about.

"I always did like interior decorating," Shay said. "Well, if that's all you need, I'd better get going."

After she had left the room, Andi frowned and turned to Jane. "'Perfect'?" she repeated. "That was another rapid turnaround on your part, wasn't it?" When her cousin shrugged, she added, "You set me up. You gave Tina a reason to leave the room just to give yourself a chance to question me about Mitch."

Jane shrugged. "Possibly. But that's one thing I haven't changed my mind about. You and Mitch. Remember what I said?"

*Maybe you both need to take this second chance.*

"Oh, I didn't forget. But it's not going to happen."

As PETE HANDED him an uncapped bottle of beer, Mitch nodded his thanks and set it down on the coffee table in the other man's living room.

Outside, the sun was hanging low, filtering through the curtains. On the other side of the room, a handful of kids played a game with blocks, toy cars and a plastic runway that seemed to involve a lot of rules.

He nodded toward a blonde five-year-old. Pete's daughter. "Rachel seems to have taken charge over Tina's and Andi's boys."

"She does that often," Pete admitted ruefully. "But I'm getting her to learn the value of sharing. I think."

He looked at Pete's son, playing happily by himself in a playpen nearby. Pete said the boy was just two, while Andi's son would soon turn three.

He'd been gone long before any of the kids had been born. Long before Andi had become a wife and mom.

He took a swig of beer, then, forcing a laugh, shook his head. "Have you got enough kids around here to keep Jed happy?"

"Ha. Not even close. At least, not close and permanent, which is the way he would like. I know he wants Andi to settle down here with her two."

"And she doesn't go along with that?"

"Doesn't seem to. According to her, she's here for the holidays and to help get the bridal business off the ground, then she's headed back home."

"Home being…"

"Arizona. Fountain Hills, Scottsdale, somewhere around there."

"Nice area, so I've heard. And steep, if you're talking Fountain Hills."

"I gather you mean money more than the elevation. That's what I hear, too. But her husband comes from money. It'll be hard for her without him, of course, but I reckon she'll be all right financially."

He nodded. Between the man's background and his responsibility to a wife and kids, Andi's husband would have been prepared to take care of his family. Mitch took a long swallow from his bottle. "It was a shock, hearing he'd gotten killed."

"Yeah." Pete shrugged. "I don't know all the details. I'm not sure anyone does."

Another family crisis Andi had kept from the rest of her family and friends. Her mother's illness. Now her husband's death. How much more would she try to handle on her own?

He knew what she was going through, knew what grief could do. He'd fought his way through it. And he wouldn't leave her to fight alone.

"What was it the boss wanted us to talk about?" Pete asked.

He shrugged. "He just thought the two of us would want to catch up. I'm glad I managed to run into you this afternoon. You can't have too much free time if you're shorthanded."

His beer halfway to his mouth, Pete paused. "What are you talking about?"

"What *Jed* and I talked about. He said you were short a few cowhands."

At that, Pete grinned and shook his head. "Your old buddy's on the payroll now, and you know he's worth any three wranglers."

Mitch and his best friend, Cole, now Tina's husband, had gone through school together. Cole had always been a hard worker and had done nothing but ranch work since they'd graduated.

The other man frowned and watched the kids play. After a few minutes, he turned back. "Did he say something about work not getting done around here?"

"No, nothing like that."

"What else did he say?"

"That you're snowed under. He asked if I'd help the

women out over at the hotel, give them a hand with moving furniture in the banquet hall, put up some of the Christmas decorations."

After a moment, Pete said, "The boys would normally help, but we've got plenty going on around the ranch to keep them busy. That's just like Jed to put another able-bodied man to work."

"He never did miss a chance to do that." He gave a rueful laugh, trying to hide the suspicions that had begun to gnaw at him.

Yeah, Jed never had liked seeing any of his boys sitting idle. But he had always been one to take care of his cowhands just as well as he cared for his family. The boss would lend a helping hand to former employees no matter how much time had passed since they'd worked on Garland Ranch.

*Damn.*

He should have realized it sooner.

True to form, his old boss wanted to help *him*. To give him a reason to feel useful.

Pride ought to make him turn down Jed's request, but doing that would also mean walking away from time with Andi.

He could see her now as clearly as he'd seen her earlier, standing in the sunshine out by the corral.

*I'm not wearing well*, she had said when he touched the fine lines near the corner of her eye. Others would have pointed out lines on their faces as proof of their troubles. Andi had just given him a laugh. One that didn't ring true.

Those small crinkles gave her face character and charm. More than that, they added maturity he didn't recognize and strength he hadn't expected. Both would make it harder to get close to her.

But he had been trained to handle tough situations.

# Chapter Six

During a busy morning spent with Tina and Jane, Andi had managed to keep her thoughts away from Mitch.

After lunch, Tina closed herself in her office to take care of the hotel bookkeeping. Jane took Robbie and Trey over to Pete's house to visit his kids and Sharon, their nanny.

Alone, Andi went into the quiet banquet hall hoping to distract herself with preparations for the wedding. She wasn't there long before she heard heavy footsteps she recognized. The sound instantly made her heart beat faster.

Groaning, she shook her head and bent over one of the cardboard cartons she had set on a folding table.

As foolish as it was, she had been almost disappointed yesterday when her path hadn't crossed with Mitch's again after he had gotten together with Pete. At dinner, Jed had mentioned seeing Mitch driving away from the ranch.

By this morning, though, she had come to her senses and acknowledged the best thing for them both would be never to see each other again.

She should have known that wouldn't happen.

She shouldn't feel this excited right now.

As Mitch strode through the doorway, she crossed

her arms, rested her hips against the table and gave in to the pleasure of seeing him. In tight black T-shirt, jeans and black biker boots, he looked taller and tougher and sexier than ever before. That T-shirt and his black hair made his eyes startling blue.

"Jed and Paz told me I would find you here."

She frowned. "Is everything okay? Do they need me to take Missy off their hands?"

"No, they're feeding her Paz's Christmas cookies, and they said that's keeping her out of trouble. They also said your kids won't ever want to go home."

Just what Jed was hoping for, she knew.

"What can I do for you?" she asked. When he grinned, she crossed her arms more tightly. "I'm very busy."

"That's why I'm here. Jed figured he'd keep *me* out of trouble by giving me a job."

She stood straighter. "I don't need a helper, thank you."

"Too late. I'm on board. What do you want me to do?"

She turned away and rummaged through a carton of ornaments. "Nothing. I've got everything under control." The words made her think again of her reaction to his kiss. Of her *loss* of control.

"Andi, walking away yesterday didn't make me go away. Pretending to be busy here doesn't mean I'll disappear. Why don't you tell me what's bothering you?"

"At the moment, you are."

"Well, that's a start."

She shot a look over her shoulder and found him smiling down at her. He was so close, she could have taken a step back and found herself in his arms. Instead, she shifted aside. "Really, Mitch, I don't need your assistance."

"Jed seems to think you do. You and Tina and Jane. And I made a promise. So that's that."

She sighed. He had made a promise. And once Grandpa made up his mind about something, that was that. As she had no choice in the matter, she might as well give in gracefully. "Fine. And I'm not pretending to be busy." She pointed to one carton. "That's what I've got on my mind right now. Decorations for the wedding. Our client requested Christmas lights. You can get started with those."

She had hoped having him work at a distance would keep him from distracting her, but she could still hear everything he said to her. Worse...or maybe better...she could see every move he made. Who knew hanging a string of lights required so much physical activity? His shoulders flexed, his biceps bulged, and she didn't even want to think about what happened to the strong muscles in his thighs as he climbed up and down the ladder.

Good thing she had acquired a helper, because she wasn't getting much work done herself.

It was a relief to hear sneakered feet pounding down the hallway. Robbie and Trey ran into the room. Naturally, Trey, who loved to climb, headed straight toward the ladder.

"Me, too! Me, too!" He reached out to Mitch, who climbed down and swung him onto his shoulder.

He wouldn't... "That's not a good—" Before she could finish her sentence, Mitch had plopped Trey onto a chair.

"You, too, Robbie," he said. "Come and watch."

Jane entered the room and came to stand beside Andi.

When both boys were seated, Mitch waved his hand in front of the window. "Okay, ready for some magic?" He inserted a plug in the nearby socket. All over the room, white fairy lights sparkled to life.

"Like stars, Mitch!" Robbie exclaimed.

"Mitch!" Trey echoed.

"Not bad at all," Jane called. In a lower voice she said to Andi, "You really ought to give that man a chance, cuz. Every woman can use a little magic in her life."

"WELL, HERE YOU ARE," Jed said from the head of the dining room table. "Just in time to join us for supper."

Andi finished settling Trey in his booster seat and reached for her utensils. As she turned to smile at the guest who had entered the room, her fingers froze around the napkin-wrapped bundle of tableware. Her smile froze, too.

Who said history didn't repeat itself?

Mitch strode through the doorway.

She had spent a very long afternoon with him in that banquet hall. Jane and the boys had stayed, and Tina had eventually joined them. Mitch had talked easily with her cousins, had given Robbie and Trey "important work" to do, and had never missed an opportunity to chat with her every time she stood still.

The last thing she needed was to deal with him again, especially in front of all her family at the dinner table.

Unfortunately, she had no say in this matter, either. Worse, when Jed directed Mitch to the empty chair beside hers, she had nowhere else to go.

He eased into his seat, then greeted her with a cool, brisk nod that made her think yet again of yesterday's anything-but-cool kiss.

"I couldn't turn down an invitation for one of Paz's home-cooked meals," he told Jed. "But don't let my mom know I said that."

"No worries, son. Your secret's safe with us."

"You have a secret?" Robbie asked.

"A secret?" Trey echoed.

"Don't we all," Mitch said.

He didn't look her way, but she felt certain he had meant the comment for her.

Rattled, she turned to the boys. "Grandpa was only teasing. There are no secrets."

"No secrets?" Robbie's eyes widened in alarm. "But Trey—"

"Not now, sweetie," Tina said quickly. "We'll talk about that later."

The Hitching Post served supper family-style, and as bowls and platters were passed, conversation turned to "have some vegetables" and "please pass the rolls."

Everyone had jumped into action to cover the slip Robbie almost made about her son's upcoming birthday parties. A slip that would have been *her* fault because she had been so distracted by Mitch.

As if he'd read her mind, he suddenly leaned closer. She tensed, until she realized he only intended to hold the heavy meat platter for her. Under cover of the voices and clanking cutlery around them, he murmured, "I wasn't teasing."

"About your mom?" she asked, pretending not to understand.

"About people keeping secrets."

"I guess you're in a good place to know." She nodded her thanks, and silently, he passed the platter along.

"It's nice to have you back here at the ranch again, Mitch," Tina said.

"It's great to be here, though I don't want to feel I'm wearing out my welcome."

This time, she refused to check whether or not he had glanced in her direction.

"No way that'll happen," Jed said. "We appreciate you giving us a hand."

*Some of us appreciate it.*

"And once the girls get this wedding stuff squared away," he added, "we need to start decorating around the hotel."

"We'll have lots of work for you to do," Tina said with a smile.

"No problem. As long as you leave me time to catch up with Jed."

"Hey, what about the rest of us?" Cole asked. "Including your best friend? I hear you talked to Pete yesterday, then forgot about tracking me down."

"We'll get together. And just to set the record straight, I don't forget people."

That sounded like a threat.

Swallowing a sigh, Andi concentrated on feeding Missy. If she insisted on reading hidden meanings into everything he said, this would be one never-ending, uncomfortable meal.

"How long are you staying in town?" Jane asked.

Andi didn't miss the way her cousin's gaze flickered from Mitch to her and back again. She also couldn't miss the fact that he sat there without saying a word. As much as she wanted to know the answer herself, she didn't like seeing him put on the spot. "I'll bet he'll stay at least long enough for the guys to have a reunion at the Cantina," she said with a laugh.

He looked at her gravely. "A reunion that's long overdue."

"I'll say," Cole agreed. "I'm holding you to it. In fact, I'll check and see if Pete and some of the other boys can make it this week. At least that way, we'll know for sure you'll be around."

"What about our open house?" Tina asked. "You'll be here through the holidays, won't you?"

"Don't know yet," Mitch said simply.

"Your daddy would like you to make this visit permanent," Jed said.

"And your mama," Paz said.

Mitch laughed. "Yeah, I'm sure they would. But my… life's in LA."

"You have a sweetheart there?" Paz asked, sounding almost dismayed.

Heart thudding, Andi kept her gaze on her plate. This time, she wouldn't jump in to save him. Yet she wasn't at all sure she wanted to know his answer.

A ridiculous reaction altogether. Considering how eager he'd been to kiss her, he couldn't have a girlfriend in LA…could he?

"No," he said. "No sweetheart."

Just the answer she wanted.

"No plans in that direction yet, either," he continued. "As I've already told Jed, there's no point in trying to get me to book the hall for a wedding. You might say I'm already married. To my job."

Just the answer she needed.

No matter how much she hated hearing him say it.

FROM HIS YEARS working on the ranch, Mitch knew the routines at the Hitching Post. After supper, the Garland family would move to the sitting room to spend time with their guests.

Preferring not to make a spectacle of himself limping along, he waited till most of the crowd left the dining room. He was just as interested in hanging back to let Andi take her seat first so he could grab one right beside her.

She sure hadn't liked seeing him walk into the room tonight or take the chair at her side. Her refusal to look his way during supper confirmed it. Her constant fiddling with knife and fork and water glass proved how nervous she felt. All those reactions had only made him more determined to get her to feel comfortable with him again.

He had thought she might grab the chance to wander away.

Instead, in the sitting room, she settled herself and Missy in an overstuffed chair close to the fireplace.

So much for sitting beside her. He took a seat on a nearby couch. "Looks like you haven't done much renovation in this room."

"We didn't change anything," she said, "besides some fresh paint. It's always cozy and welcoming in here."

That it was, from the overstuffed chairs and couches covered with Paz's bright handmade afghans to the old rocker pulled up close to the hearth. On the wall across from him, a clock gave a slow, steady *tick-tock*. Over in one corner of the room, Robbie and Trey galloped toy horses across a low wooden table.

Trey must have caught his glance. He waved. "Look! Horse. Bi-i-ig horse, Mitch."

"I see that. Just like the one you ride."

"Yeah." Trey laughed, then turned back to Robbie.

Jed came to take Andi's daughter from her. Mitch saw the smile she gave her grandfather. It lit her face, reminding him of the smiles she'd once sent his way.

Holding the baby in one arm, the older man took a seat beside him on the couch.

"Later on, Jed, when your hands aren't so full, maybe you and I could get together about what else I can do for you around here."

Jed waved his free hand. "Aw, relax. You're a guest here tonight. Besides, this is family time." He turned slightly to show off the baby. "Cute little thing, isn't she?"

"She is. I remember Laurie being that small. Heck, I can remember all my brothers and sisters at that stage."

"And I bet you never let 'em forget it."

He laughed. "I do like to remind them, the boys especially, of all the times I saw them running around in diapers."

"Changed those diapers, too, I'd reckon, knowing Lyle."

"Yeah, that was one of the drawbacks of being the oldest. Dad put me through my paces, no matter how much I protested."

"Good training for you. You'll make a good daddy, then. Won't he, Andi?"

She started, as if her thoughts had been far away from the sitting room. Still, she didn't miss a beat. "As you said, Grandpa, we know his father. I'd imagine Sheriff Weston has Mitch well-trained for almost anything."

She'd stressed those final two words. Why, he couldn't tell. When she raised her chin, he couldn't read that, either. Defiance? Determination? Challenge?

Was she thinking about yesterday, when he had kissed her?

He had told her the kiss was to show her neither of them had forgotten their past. *Yeah, right.* That had been the handiest excuse he could grab on to to explain his heat-of-the-moment response.

The truth was, after seeing the pity in her eyes, he had acted out of pure gut instinct, kissing her to prove he was well on the way to being himself again. And he had succeeded.

Just in case she had started to think he was hinting about the future, at supper tonight, he had made it clear he didn't have any plans to settle down. But at this point, he couldn't swear whether he'd meant the announcement as a caution to her or reassurance for himself.

All he knew was, he'd need to try like heck to avoid any potentially hot moments.

# Chapter Seven

"Nice hideaway."

Startled by the familiar voice, Andi jumped. Her sharp scissors almost punctured the package she was attempting to open. She set aside the order of candy-covered almonds destined for wedding favors. Mitch stood there leaning against the door frame. She glared at him. "This isn't a hideaway. And was it necessary for you to sneak up on me like that?"

"I didn't sneak. You should be more aware of what's going on around you."

He had a point, considering she had sat there so deep in contemplation, she hadn't heard his approach. Worse, though she had left the sitting room intending to put space between them, she hadn't been able to escape her thoughts.

"I didn't read you as someone antisocial enough to go off and leave her family," he said.

"I didn't leave them. They're in good hands. Literally, in my daughter's case."

When he and Grandpa had gotten involved in conversation, she had checked to make sure Grandpa hadn't wanted to turn Missy over to her. Not much chance of that. Experience had taught her Jed wouldn't give up any opportunity to cuddle his only great-granddaughter.

A quick look across the room had shown Trey engrossed in playing with Robbie and his toy horses.

It was safe for her to slip quietly from the sitting room without anyone noticing. Or so she had thought.

When Mitch closed the door to the suite, she felt both a rush of annoyance and a shiver of anticipation. She didn't know which upset her more. But she shouldn't have *any* feelings when it came to him.

"Speaking of your family," he said, "what was all that at the supper table about secrets?"

"Robbie almost spilled the beans about Trey's surprise birthday parties."

"Parties, as in more than one?"

"Yes. The kids and I are going back home to celebrate with my mother-in-law and the rest of her family on Trey's actual birthday. After that, we'll have my family party here at the hotel. But that can't be why you're up here now. What can I do for you?" she asked as levelly as she could.

He glanced around him. "I also didn't read you as someone who'd hide away in a hotel bridal suite. Unless, of course, you were waiting for your groom."

The thought of Mitch playing that role made her entire body overheat. Flustered, she snapped, "I told you, this isn't a hideaway. Jane and Tina and I are organizing for the wedding, and we decided we needed a better temporary workstation than Tina's small office downstairs. Besides, we figured one of the suites would give us more privacy."

"It does that."

"Obviously not as much as we thought. How did you know where to find me?"

"I'm a cop, remember?"

"How could I forget? But that doesn't answer my question."

"Tina gave me the heads-up you might have come here."

*"Tina?"* It was bad enough Jane had already begun pushing her in a direction she didn't want to go. But why would her quiet younger cousin have gotten involved? Tina didn't know anything about her summer with Mitch. "Is she on her way up here?"

"No. And it sounded like she and Jane were finished working for the night. I guess you're an overachiever."

"Officially, I'm the hotel's interim wedding planner while they look for someone to hire permanently. Grandpa's already upset we had our first wedding party cancel a couple of months ago. And it was a wedding I'd booked. So I've got to make sure this one's a big success."

He crossed the room to sit on the king-size bed within arm's reach of the desk chair. Immediately, she rose. She couldn't have changed seats at supper, but she had managed to slip away from the sitting room. And she could certainly leave the suite now.

He stretched his leg in front of him and sucked in a breath through clenched teeth. Concern froze her in place. "Are you okay?"

"Fine."

"What happened, Mitch?"

"I sat too long, and it stiffened up on me."

"That's not what I meant, and you know it." Concern gave way to frustration. "You question me like you're a cop—"

"I *am* a cop."

"Yes, I know. But I don't like being treated like a suspect. And I don't like when you want to know things about me, yet never give back anything yourself."

"It seems to me we've got a lot more history to discuss than my bum knee."

"You mean the fact we hadn't forgotten each other, don't you? We *should* forget those memories. We're better off letting them stay in the past."

"That's not what I'm getting at this time."

He rested his hand on her forearm. Despite her frustration, she couldn't ignore the pleasurable chill his touch sent through her.

"I think you've got something else on your mind. Other worries. Other memories, maybe. And we've already seen how they can come back to haunt us."

*Haunt* was the right word. Meeting Mitch again had instantly reignited their teenage passion. Their first love. But his injury and his claim of being married to his job in Los Angeles were both painful reminders of what she *had* to put behind her. She had to make it clear to him, once and for all, that she'd gotten over their past.

"I've made other memories that take the place of ours." *More lies.* Though she had found a new life, nothing could take the place of those memories she had created with Mitch. But she couldn't tell him that. "I've had two children. I lost my husband—"

"I know that."

"No, you don't. Not all of it."

"That's just my point."

He took her hand. Her mind warned her to pull free, but as he tugged gently, her emotions refused to listen. She sank to the bed beside him, making sure to keep space between them and still, she fought to keep from sliding closer.

"That summer, we talked about everything, Andi. All I want is for you to talk to me now the way you did then. Tell me what happened. After that, you'll be able to put those memories away in some neat, little box—like a Christmas present. Or like that package over there." He gestured to the desk.

She took another unsteady breath.

Obviously, he did a better job than she did of tuning in to the surroundings. She hadn't thought he had even noticed the package.

She shook her head. "I lost my husband. He went to work one day and never came home. That's all." She had the right to keep her story to herself, the way he guarded his. It had to be related to his injury and why he had come home. She tugged her hand free. "You need to leave, Mitch. I respect what you and everyone in law enforcement do. But there's no way I'll get close to someone in such a dangerous job."

"We're already close. We're friends. Don't think about what I do. Think of me as the boy you once knew."

"You're not a boy, you're a man—"

"Glad you noticed." He gave her a crooked smile.

"—and I'm a woman—"

"No argument there."

"—with responsibilities." Why did her voice have to shake? "*Lots* of responsibilities," she ended firmly.

"And I respect you for that. But there's no way I'm going to walk away when I think you need to talk. And I hope you'll tell me the truth."

"I don't—"

"Yeah, you don't lie. I've heard that before, a million times, from people who couldn't make an honest confession if I dictated it to them. But never from you. And I know you want to set a good example for your kids. Then be responsible now," he said, "and give me straight answers."

Sighing, she shook her head. "You won't give up, will you?"

"You don't want me to, do you? Because you know talking to me might help."

He wrapped his arm around her shoulders, his touch gentle, almost brotherly, yet her heart pounded even as her breathing seemed to shut down.

When she turned to look at him, he reached up to brush her hair away from her face. Their eyes met. Their gazes held. They were so close, and in an instant she was standing outside at the corral again. Just as she had then, she instinctively tilted her head, nestling her cheek against his palm.

Did he move closer, or did she? She couldn't have said. All she knew was they met somewhere in the middle, and when he lowered his mouth to hers, she returned his kiss as eagerly as she always had that one summer.

No matter what she had said, they weren't a man and a woman now, not in her mind. They were a boy and a girl again. A couple of teens in love, making out in the hayloft or beside a summer-swollen creek or inside a honeymoon cabin not far from the hotel.

Just a couple of teens on their own…

But not alone. Not when she could hear footsteps in the hallway.

Backing away, she brushed at her lips with one hand and smoothed her hair with the other. They had never been discovered during any of their make-out sessions. How ironic to be caught now.

The sound of footsteps, many footsteps, thudded on the wooden floorboards. They grew louder as what sounded like an army of people approached the suite… reached the doorway…

And passed by.

She let out a sigh of relief.

"I didn't mean for that to happen—" he began.

"Neither did I—" Then why wasn't she sorry? "—but we both know it can't happen again. Mitch, you have to leave."

"Now?" He frowned and leaned back, using his elbows to prop himself up on the bed.

She fought the urge to throw herself on him just as the teenage Andi would have done. Judging by the way his jeans tented in front, that could be both a very satisfying and a very stupid move. She had no time in her life for either.

Instead, she returned to sit at the desk.

"Things were just getting interesting," he protested.

She could hear the forced amusement in his voice. He was trying to laugh this off, to make less of it, probably in an attempt to leave her feeling better about this mistake...about this *kiss* that never should have happened.

"Maybe things were getting interesting for you," she said as lightly as she could manage. "But I'm not interested, thank you." *Liar.* She was intrigued. Fascinated. Ready for more. But she shouldn't be.

She reached for the package and the scissors, hanging on to them tightly as if they would help fend off Mitch's advances...not that he was making any at the moment.

She risked a look over her shoulder.

He raised a brow.

Again she struggled, this time to swallow all the questions she could barely hold back. How could they have reached this moment of mutual temporary insanity? Worse, how could she have given in to it? And how could he sit there looking at her so coolly when she was burning up inside and out?

"Not interested, huh? You could have fooled me."

If only she could have tricked herself. But that was impossible when her reactions were so easy to define. She wasn't simply recalling a teen's faraway memories. She was feeling here-and-now emotions without having a clue how to handle them. No, she might not be able to fool herself, but she certainly was acting like a fool.

"Mitch. We can't continue this conversation here. We can't *be* here. We're lucky the people who passed by weren't headed for this suite. Please, go—before anyone else comes along."

Slowly, he rose to his feet. Deliberately, she knew, he adjusted his jeans. "You can feel sorry for me and my limp all you want at the moment, because it won't be my knee making me hobble out of here."

Feel *sorry* for him? No, sympathy certainly wasn't on her long list of emotions. Clutching the scissors so tightly her fingers went numb, she watched him walk slowly across the room.

At the doorway, he turned back. "I'm leaving for now," he said, "but that doesn't mean we've wrapped things up."

"Coffee's up," Deputy Hernandez announced.

"Sounds good."

Mitch propped his leg on a desk in the outer office of Cowboy Creek's sheriff's department and lost himself in the memory of last night.

Once Tina had filled him in on Andi's possible whereabouts, he'd gone up to the suite only to talk. Even taking her hand and putting his arm around her had been meant as reassuring gestures, nothing more. His aim was to find out what was bothering her. To help her, not to come on to her like the oversexed adolescent he'd once been.

But touching her cheek had done him in. Watching her tilt her head as if seeking more of that touch had made him lose control. Before he had known what was happening, he had gotten so carried away, he'd pushed aside thoughts of his goal. Hell, he'd forgotten he had one.

She seemed to have that effect on him.

He had to forget about that, too. Had to put his teenage hormones on hold if he was ever going to help her. But besides frustrating him to death, what good would that do? She would never open up to him with all of her family and the hotel guests within earshot. The way she had insisted he leave the suite—in his condition, no less—had proven that.

"Here you go." Paco set the foam cup on the desk beside Mitch. "Black okay with you?"

He nodded at the coffee cup. "Black's fine. Back home, we don't have the luxury of making it light. Or sweet." He grinned at Paco. "Depending on whose turn it was to stock the kitchen supply cabinet, we're lucky to find a few packets of fake sugar wedged into a crack in the shelf."

"Same here," Paco said. He took the chair behind the desk. "I guess you big-city cops aren't so different from us, huh?"

Mitch nodded in the spirit of solidarity. The desk phone rang, and as the deputy answered the call, he glanced around the office again.

Not much had changed in here for years.

Growing up, he had made plenty of visits to the office with his dad. In those days, this room had seemed so much bigger, so much more exciting than it did now. Maybe he'd outgrown it. Or more likely, he'd grown used to a different place.

Still, the office looked familiar. Comfortable. All law enforcement offices might feel the same way. He wouldn't know, as he'd gone straight from school to the LAPD.

Paco hung up the phone. "Routine call. Miz Greta's cat is on the loose again."

They both laughed.

"I'll bet you see more action in LA."

"Sometimes, sometimes not. We get our share of animal rescue calls."

"And break-ins and shootings and drug busts." Paco sounded almost envious.

"Yeah, those, too. There's a lot to be said for peace and quiet, though."

"We get plenty of that."

"I'll tell you one thing we don't get, at least in my area. That's cattle rustlers."

"Yeah, I'll bet. We still run into them, but not too often. Your dad got a reputation for clamping down on that around here—" Paco laughed "—after he drop-kicked the last wannabe rustler in the creek."

"I never heard that one." What else had he missed that a flying visit and a few-times-a-year phone call didn't cover? "That was a while ago?"

"Years," Paco said firmly. "And we haven't had a problem in that line since. Your dad's a good man."

A while later, once he'd left the office and started a slow walk up Canyon Road toward home, Mitch thought of that comment again.

Lately, he hadn't lived up to his old man's high standards. His former boss was telling stories to help him save face. He'd let himself down again last night by losing his ability to keep his hands off Andi.

At the moment, he didn't have much going for him. The one thing he had to hang on to was his determination to follow his instincts.

If he couldn't trust himself to do that, he wasn't worthy of wearing a badge.

# Chapter Eight

"Well, we're making progress," Jane announced.

Andi looked up from the pile of red netting she was cutting into rectangles. "We are?"

Tina sat at the desk in the honeymoon suite going through their wedding checklist.

Jane knelt on the floor poring over photos she had taken of sample place settings they had designed for this first wedding. "Sure," she said. "We've moved on from picking out fabric patterns to finalizing settings and party favors—now that Bridezilla has finally started making some decisions."

Andi rolled her eyes. "Her name's Sandra. You've got to stop calling her that, Jane. When she gets here for the wedding, I'm liable to open my mouth and say the wrong thing."

"Not you, sweet cousin," Jane mocked.

"Don't squabble, girls," Tina said. "And look at the bright side. We're on budget and a week ahead of schedule."

"Spoken like a true accountant."

Andi glared at Jane, then turned to Tina. "That's true. Double kudos to you." She hoped her smile didn't look as strained as it felt. During the past few days, instead of progress, she had felt only pressure from every direction.

Jed had so many hopes riding on relaunching the Hitching Post's bridal business. This wedding had to be a success, to generate word-of-mouth referrals and bring in new reservations. It had—as Grandpa had often said lately—to go off without a hitch.

Mitch had shown up at the hotel every day this week and without a murmur of protest had helped with anything they requested. He had repositioned tables and chairs in the banquet hall, brought down boxes of Christmas decorations from the attic and strung lights in the lobby and sitting room.

He had also kept the conversation rolling, had kept the kids occupied once they started getting underfoot, and had even managed to keep Jed from trying to climb a ladder to hang some of the decorations.

He had somehow done all this without once being out of her line of sight...or maybe she had just spent too much time watching him.

Yesterday, Jane had jokingly told him he could have Sundays off, yet he had returned this morning for brunch.

Each day he had acted as if nothing had ever happened between them, while she still dreamed of the kiss they had shared on this very bed. The kiss she wanted to repeat.

*I'm leaving for now,* Mitch had said before walking out of this room that night, *but that doesn't mean we've wrapped things up.*

His parting words only added to her stress.

He kept insisting she talk to him, that she had something bothering her. And she did. But their kiss and her response had only added to her list of worries.

She even felt pressure from her own son. Maybe because of their conversation about their "badges," Trey seemed to have latched on to Mitch. He had insisted on carrying his booster seat over to the chair on the opposite side of Mitch's. When they had all moved to the sitting room, he trailed after the man like one of Robbie's miniature cars on a string. And the latest new words in his vocabulary? *"Mitch... Mitch... Mitch."*

Her son's growing attachment worried her more than anything else could.

Beside her on the mattress, her cell phone buzzed with the special ringtone she had set for their client's messages.

"Now, if only Bridezilla would stop texting you every three minutes," Jane said, "we could get everything wrapped up."

Andi glared. "Would you *please* not call her that?"

Tina closed her laptop. "Why don't we quit? It's almost dinnertime." On Sundays, the Hitching Post offered only two meals, brunch and a midafternoon Sunday dinner. "I need to see if Abuela needs help. Cole mentioned taking all the kids into town for ice cream after dinner. I think we should go along, too."

"Ice cream?" Jane said. "It's December."

Tina laughed. "The kids don't care about that. And you're not in New York, anymore, remember? It's not nearly as cold here."

"True. Then count me in."

Andi nodded. "It *is* a good idea. I'll be with you in a minute. I just need to check my phone." She hesitated. With everything else bothering her, she didn't need an argument with Jane on her conscience. "The text was from…the woman we will now refer to as you-know-who."

To her relief, Jane and Tina laughed.

As she watched them both leave the room, she cradled the cell phone in her hands. Nothing would excuse the way she had responded to her cousin, but she had to admit she knew the cause.

Since her encounter with Mitch in this very room, her nerves had felt as tight as a high-tension wire. At Jane's comment, the wire had snapped. Her cousin had been right when she'd mentioned wrapping things up. Right in more ways than she knew.

That's what *she* needed to do—with Mitch. To wrap things up between them once and for all.

She couldn't get involved with him.

For her children's sake, she needed to let go and move on.

Yet the worst of the pressure she'd felt these past few days had come from inside her.

Seeing Mitch here provided a constant reminder that she had once loved him. That she still couldn't resist him. And that, instead of wrapping up their relationship, she wanted to pick up from where they had left off.

MITCH STOOD NEAR the Big Dipper's front counter patiently waiting his turn to pay for his ice cream cone. With Andi right in front of him, he was in no rush to move the line along.

Earlier that morning, though he was off duty according to Jane, he had made the trip out to the Hitching Post. He didn't want to admit it, but he was hoping for more time alone with Andi. Not for a repeat of the night he had found her upstairs in the suite, but for the chance to talk.

After brunch, when she had left the sitting room and hadn't returned, Jed mentioned she had gone upstairs again. She was in the middle of wedding preparations. With Jane and Andi.

After a final cup of coffee, he had wandered by the suite, where she'd made a point of indicating how busy they all were. His certainty she was avoiding him had been confirmed both by the look on her face when she'd seen him waiting in the Big Dipper and by the way she was attempting to ignore him now.

And after what had happened between them the other night, maybe she had the right idea.

So far, she'd given him only a glance, quick and colder than the double scoop of rocky road he planned to order.

"Didn't expect to see me here, did you?" he asked over her shoulder. Their eyes met in the mirrored panel on the wall behind the cash register. Hers still looked a frosty blue.

"I'll bet you didn't expect to be here," she countered.

He laughed. "You win. Cole must have told you. At first, when he called to get together here in town, I thought he meant the Cantina. Then he mentioned taking the kids to the Big Dipper." And *then* he'd said Tina and Jane and Andi were also coming along. Suddenly, an afternoon at the ice cream parlor sounded even better than a night out with the boys. "I figured I'd take him up on the invitation."

"Why?"

"Why?" He sure couldn't tell her the truth, that despite all the warnings he'd given himself, he'd wanted to see her again. "Because I like ice cream."

When it was her turn to order at the counter, he said, "I've got this." Once he'd ordered, he reached around her to take his cone from Shay, the clerk. His arm brushed Andi's shoulder, and he thought again of the way he had held her that night. He handed Shay a twenty. "Keep the change."

"Better check to make sure it's not counterfeit," Andi said.

He leaned around her to meet her eyes. "Hey, I work on the right side of the law, remember?"

"How could I ever forget?"

She grabbed a handful of napkins from the dispenser, and they moved away from the counter.

The folks of Cowboy Creek had turned out in force tonight. The place was packed. Cole and the rest of their group sat around a couple of tables.

"No seats in our corner," he said, attempting to hide a smile. Much as he liked Jed's clan, he didn't at all mind this chance to get Andi to himself. Maybe to finally get her to open up to him.

"It looks like there aren't any seats anywhere," she said, scanning the room.

"Guess we'll have to go out front."

She waved to the group in the corner and pointed to the door. They all smiled and waved back.

He trailed her outside to a table. Fortunately, it was on the sidewalk opposite the side of the shop where her family sat. At least he wouldn't have the Garland clan sharing a play-by-play of the action.

He took a seat beside her and gestured at her cone. "What is that, anyway, plain old vanilla?"

She nodded.

"A poor choice compared to mine."

"You think so?" She shrugged. "I don't much care for that bumpy stuff you're eating."

"You mean rocky road."

"'Bumpy stuff,'" she repeated. "That's what Robbie calls it, so of course Trey calls it that, too."

"Nice kids," he said. "I'll bet you're happy they're getting so much time together now you've come for a visit. Trey's happy, I can tell you that. He definitely looks up to Robbie."

She froze with her ice cream halfway to her mouth.

Slowly, she lowered her hand again and began fiddling with the paper wrapped around the cone.

"What's the matter?" he asked quietly.

She shrugged again. "Just thinking."

He thought, too, back to what he had said. Maybe this would be the opening he'd been waiting for. "I'll bet your son looked up to his dad. Most boys do. How is he dealing with what happened to your husband?"

"He's fine." The chill he'd heard in her voice earlier had returned. "He's too young to be aware of things."

"What will you tell him when he asks where his dad is?"

"I don't know. I'll face that when it happens."

"Well, you're right. He *is* young." Young enough to forget, something he wished he could say about himself. "That's a point in his favor."

*"Favor?"* She shot a glance at him, then looked past him into the distance.

Her level stare told him she wasn't noticing the sun-drenched sidewalk, the strolling pedestrians or the Sunday drivers coasting along Canyon Road.

He could feel her shutting down. Slipping away. He wanted her back. "Kids Trey's age can easily mix up reality with what they see on the cartoons. Plus they're resilient. They bounce back from things that hit adults like a ton of bricks. That's all I meant. Sorry for sounding too blunt."

"That comes with being a cop, doesn't it? Because you're used to dealing with tragedy."

"Not as much as people think. For sure, not as much as they see on TV."

"But you face it more than most people do."

He gripped the cone in his hand. How had she managed to spin the questions back his way? "Yeah, we all see our share of life's worst moments."

"How bad was yours?"

He shook his head. "Nothing we need to discuss. Let's just stick to the first topic. We were talking about your boy."

"No, you were leading up to talking about my husband, and I was avoiding falling into your trap."

"Trap?"

"Another one of your interrogations."

"I wasn't interrogating you, Andi."

"It felt that way," she said sadly. "Tonight and the other times you've asked questions. You want to find out what happened in my past. What happened with Grant. But when I ask about your past, about how you got hurt, you change the subject."

She had kept her voice pitched low, and still he felt uneasy. He wasn't used to being on the receiving end of a grilling. He wasn't ready to talk about what had gone down in LA.

He spotted a trash can a few feet from them. Leaning over, he sent his ice cream cone into the kill zone. "This isn't the place or time to get into that."

"Then where is the place? And when will it be time?"

He shrugged and said simply, "I don't know." Because *nowhere* and *never* wouldn't satisfy her.

# Chapter Nine

Mitch tipped back his bottle and took what should have been a cold, refreshing slug of beer. Cold, yeah, the Cantina had that covered. He couldn't blame them for the drink not measuring up to the rest.

At this point, nothing could refresh him. He was as worn-out as the oily rag he used to clean his firearms.

To hell with the dangerous job Andi liked to throw up to him. To hell and back with the bullet he'd taken in his knee. His relationship with her was going to do him in.

From just a few yards away, a jukebox blared. In the booth opposite him, Pete Brannigan looked at his watch. They were waiting for Cole and a couple of their other friends to show up. "They ought to be getting here soon. I bet it'll be good to see some of the guys from school. Cole said you might even make it out to the ranch for Jed's party."

"I don't know about that." Who knew where he'd be a couple of weeks down the road. Between now and then, he had the follow-up appointments with the surgeon and the department shrink. He had a lot riding on those appointments. Too much. Right now, he couldn't risk thinking about the outcome.

He didn't want to think about where things might stand with Andi by that time, either.

He took another slug of beer and thought again about his lack of progress with Andi. He'd tried to talk with her—despite her accusation about his questions. Half the time he'd said anything remotely personal about her, she had switched the conversation to something else. The other half of the time, she'd tried to get him to open up.

Talk about interrogation. She had a damned good technique herself.

He looked up to find Pete frowning at him. "You're not drinking tequila," Pete said, "so I don't guess you've swallowed a worm. But you sure look like it. What's up?"

He shrugged. "Thinking about some things I've been working on. I've hit a brick wall."

The other man shook his head sympathetically. "That's rough."

"Yeah." He sat back, ready for some diversion from his thoughts. He had seen the front door open and Cole enter the bar. If anyone could distract him, his best friend could. He lifted his bottle in greeting.

Pete rose. "My shout."

As he walked away, Cole slid into the vacant seat and said, "I'm late. Got out of the shower and found Robbie sitting on the edge of the bed, waiting for a heart-to-heart. Maybe you need one, too. You've been walking around lately looking like a bear with a thorn in his butt. Pete will be back with the beers soon, so let's not waste time. What's up?"

"Nothing." He scowled. First Pete picking up on his mood, and now Cole. He could kiss his undercover work goodbye if he didn't do a better job at hiding his thoughts.

Another problem he could attribute to Andi.

"You ought to settle down, have a kid or two." Cole grinned. "It could help your disposition."

"There's nothing wrong with my disposition. But,

what—you've been a daddy less than a year, and already you've found it's the cure for everything?"

"Close to it." Cole suddenly sobered. "Being a family man gives you a new perspective."

*So does watching your partner die.*

"And," Cole went on, "I know where you can find a ready-made family."

Andi and her kids.

"She's leaving tomorrow, going home for a couple of days, but then she'll be back. You couldn't do any better, Mitch. Andi's one in a million. And those kids of hers would only sweeten the deal."

At the thought of Trey and his *"Bi-i-ig horse, Mitch!"* he had trouble holding back a smile. He gulped his beer to ease the sudden tightness in his throat. A family didn't fit his lifestyle. Besides, Andi wouldn't smile at him two days in a row. She would hardly settle down with him. "Not interested, thanks. Why would I want a wife and kids when I'd never be around to spend time with them?"

"My thought, too. But I finally saw the light."

He shrugged. "The only thing I see is Pete coming back with our beers."

AT GARLAND RANCH the next morning, Mitch parked his truck near the corral in the spot he'd begun to think of as his.

Across the yard, he saw Cole sitting on the Hitching Post's porch rail, more than likely watching for him.

Later on last evening, he had turned over what Cole had said to him about Andi. Especially the part about her leaving town. In a phone call afterward, he had asked a few pointed questions. With luck, by now his best friend had gotten some answers.

Now he walked up to the other man, who clapped him

on the shoulder. "About time. C'mon, let's go inside. I told Tina you called last night because you wanted to stop in for breakfast."

"*Breakfast?* That's the best reason you could come up with?"

"What's wrong with it? You've been around here for almost every meal lately, anyhow." Cole laughed and headed up to the porch. "Tina and Jane think you and Andi ought to get together."

Mitch stumbled, almost missing the next step.

For a split second, he thought his leg would let him down—literally. But he managed to grab the rail and continue up the steps a couple of beats behind Cole, who appeared not to have noticed.

"Did they volunteer that all on their own, or did you ask them?"

On the porch, Cole came to a halt and hung his head in mock shame. "They grilled Pete and me about what went on at the Cantina last night."

"And you coughed up."

"I didn't say anything about whipping your butt at the pool table."

"Well, thanks for that."

"You *ought* to be thankful, old friend. I could have ruined your reputation."

*Got that taken care of.*

"And I didn't say anything about our heart-to-heart or the way you blasted my suggestion. But I've got a feeling you didn't mind the idea as much as you tried to let on."

"What does that mean?"

"It means I don't think you're completely rejecting the idea of getting together with Andi. How could I, after your phone call?"

"And you've coughed that up to the women *and* Pete?"

"Not a single word. But I still managed to get the info you wanted."

"Where is it?"

"Right here." From his pocket, Cole pulled out a slip of paper and handed it over.

He nodded his thanks. "Save me a seat in the dining room. I'll be there in a few minutes. First, I've got to make a call."

"I'll bet you do." Laughing, Cole walked away.

Mitch he took a deep breath and went over to the porch swing.

He had no delusions about a relationship with Andi. But he still had a goal to reach. Wasn't that why he'd called Cole last night and why he'd come here to have things out with Andi this morning?

He thumbed open the folded sheet of paper and stared down at the details of her flights to and from Phoenix.

Then he pulled his cell phone from his pocket. He was taking a risk—a big one—but what did that matter? This might be the only chance he would ever have to be completely alone with Andi.

"I'LL BE LEAVING soon for the airport."

Andi laughed. "Not too soon," she said into her cell phone. Cara, her best friend forever—and now also her kids' babysitter—would pick the three of them up in Phoenix for the drive to her mother-in-law's in Fountain Hills. She was looking forward to staying with Cara tonight, sharing girl talk and catching up. "I know it's a short flight, but we haven't even left the Hitching Post yet."

"I just can't wait to see you and the kids again. It's been a long couple of weeks."

That was an understatement.

"Are you done packing yet?"

She looked down at the small pile of clothing on the bed and laughed again. "Almost. It's just for one night. It's not like I have that much to bring with me. Two bags and the kids' car seats, that's it."

"You'll have a lot more with you after Trey's party, I'll bet."

"I'm sure I will. Ginnie and the rest of Grant's family have always been so generous with gifts for the kids." Her mother-in-law had asked especially to have Trey's party at her house on his actual birthday. "I won't bring my package for Trey, since I'd just have to carry it back here again. I'll give it to him at my family's party tomorrow night."

"You're still okay with leaving the kids at her house and coming to stay with me?"

Cara knew all her worries about Grant's family, but they both also knew Ginnie was a wonderful grandmother. "Of course I'm okay with it. We're overdue for some BFF time. And I'm glad Ginnie wants to keep Trey and Missy overnight."

When they finished the call, she dropped the cell phone onto the bed near her purse.

At the time Ginnie had asked to keep the kids the night of Trey's birthday, Andi had been grateful for the chance to work some overtime at the dress shop.

Now, here she was staying in Cowboy Creek and grateful for the opportunity to leave, even if only for a day. It would give her some breathing space, some time to be on her own without worrying about running into Mitch.

A knock sounded on the door. "Come on in," she called, folding up the sweatshirt Trey might need for the airplane.

She heard the door open and close again immediately. Frowning, she turned.

Mitch stood leaning against the door.

She clutched the sweatshirt in an automatic reflex triggered half by happiness at seeing him and half by apprehension. "What are you doing here so early?"

"I came for breakfast—"

"The dining room's downstairs." When he grinned and headed toward her, her heart gave an extra little beat.

"Very funny. As I was saying, I came for breakfast and was surprised you weren't there."

"I'm packing."

He looked past her. "Yeah, I can see that."

"How did you know where I was?"

"You were the only one not at the breakfast table, so I deduced I might find you here. Trey told me the other day which room he was staying in."

She turned back to the bed. "Well, I don't know that entertaining you in our hotel room is such a good idea."

"Did you plan to entertain me?"

"Oh, you're very amusing, too, aren't you?"

"Believe it or not, I can be, in the right circumstances." He stood behind her just as he had at the ice cream parlor. Now, just as then, a tingling awareness ran through her. "But we haven't had the right circumstances for much of anything."

"We managed," she said drily, crossing her arms and turning to face him. She hadn't realized he had taken another step toward her. Her forearms brushed his chest, and she would have sworn an electrical charge passed through her.

She didn't lose her balance. She wasn't a bit unsteady on her feet. And still, instinct or memory or familiarity made her reach out to him just as he reached for her.

Every sense seemed heightened, more alert. The warmth of his hands on her shoulders made her melt like a scoop of softened ice cream. The heat of his mouth on hers made her hot all over. She tugged on his T-shirt, wanting him closer. Wanting more. This was no boy-and-girl kiss, no revival of old memories. This was forging new memories. This was taking a risk.

This was crazy.

She backed away, or as far away as she could with the bed planted behind her. "Mitch, we can't—"

"I know. We can't do this here. We can't talk in the suite upstairs. We can't avoid all the hotel guests and we can't get any space from your family. But I know where we can do all that."

"Where?" she blurted.

"Arizona."

*"What?"* She couldn't have heard his response. She darn well wouldn't give away how breathless the suggestion had left her. "We can't."

"Why not? We need to talk."

"Talk?" Her senses were still reeling. But she felt sure talk wasn't the only thing on Mitch's agenda. She tried to ignore her shiver of pleasure at the thought, to forget about what he might have meant and focus on what he had actually said. The idea of conversation—of *talking*–with Mitch made her pause.

If they were completely alone with no fear of anyone breaking in on them, would he finally open up and tell her what had happened to him?

If they were completely alone—

"We need some time together."

He seemed to have read her mind, although considering the jumbled state of her emotions, she wouldn't have been surprised to learn her expression had given her away.

She swallowed hard. They stood so close, she had nowhere else to look—nowhere else she *wanted* to look—but into his clear blue eyes. Obviously, he did plan more than just conversation. She couldn't deny how much she wanted that, too.

But once they had crossed that line, would she be able to cross back again?

"Andi, we need the right place to talk, and that danged sure isn't here."

"I'm leaving for the airport in just a few minutes."

"I know that. So am I."

Her jaw dropped. "You're riding with us?"

He shook his head. "No. At breakfast, Jed mentioned someone needed to give you a lift. I volunteered to take you to the airport. And then, if you're willing, I'd like to go with you to Phoenix."

Her heartbeat went into triple time. She had to force herself to protest. "I'm only going overnight."

"And you're leaving the kids at your mother-in-law's for a sleepover."

She swallowed a gasp. "How do you know?"

"Jed mentioned that, too."

There was no way now she could mistake what he was asking, what he wanted. Something much riskier than their kiss. They might have only this one chance...

"One night," he murmured. "Before we say goodbye once and for all."

Her breath caught at the thought of never seeing him again. She already had too many sad memories, too many things she couldn't go back in time to change. But she could fix this. She could end things between them on a better note than she had before. She could finally satisfy the need—*her* need—to make up for walking away from him.

He lifted his hand to her cheek.

As always, she tilted her head and nestled against his palm. "One night," she whispered.

And one chance that could lead to something more.

# Chapter Ten

From the driver's seat of their rental car, Mitch could look into the rearview mirror and see both Trey and Missy strapped into their seats. A better view than the one to his right, where Andi sat staring through the front windshield without seeing a thing, he'd bet.

"Look, Mitch," Trey yelled from the rear seat, pointing to the designs carved into the highway's retaining wall. "Bi-i-ig lizards!"

"I see them, buddy. There are lots of them, aren't there?"

"Yeah. Bi-i-ig lizards. And bi-i-ig trees."

On their ride to Fountain Hills, the kid pointed out the planes banking toward them, the palm trees in the distance and every single lizard they passed. Trey's chatter helped fill the silence from Andi's corner of the car.

When she had finally agreed to let him accompany her on this trip, he couldn't help the rush of satisfaction that thrummed through him. Sealing the deal with another kiss had left him certain she wanted him along, too.

But at the car rental counter waiting for their vehicle, she voiced her concerns about how her in-laws were going to take his presence. Then the attendant had presented their paperwork, and they hadn't had time to finish the discussion.

She had most likely spent the ride to her mother-in-law's trying to come up with a plan.

Their midafternoon arrival spared them from heavy traffic. "What happened to that Phoenix rush hour I've heard people complain about?"

"We didn't miss it by much," she said. "Turn at that next corner, after the big saguaro."

"Bi-i-ig cactus," Trey yelled.

Mitch grinned, and Andi smiled.

He coasted along a wide curved drive and stopped the rental in front of a three-story stucco building the size of a small castle.

A concrete walkway led to a towering, metal-girded double door sporting Christmas wreaths larger than the tires on his truck. The door could easily have been plucked from an abandoned castle on the moors. A moat and drawbridge wouldn't have looked out of place, either.

No doubt about it, Andi's husband's family had some bucks.

He released Trey from his car seat, then went to the trunk to collect the bag Andi had said held the kids' overnight clothes.

By the time she had taken the baby into her arms and joined him near the trunk of the car, she was more than ready to talk.

"How are we going to explain my bringing you along with me?" She had kept her voice low for the kids' sake, he was sure.

"You having second thoughts?" he asked. Better to find out now, to regroup if necessary.

Her steady gaze gave him the answer before she replied. "No, I'm not."

"Good. No worries, then," he said in the calm, measured tone that often came in handy on the job. Andi had called her mother-in-law from the airport and asked to bring a guest. "I'm an old friend of your family's from Cowboy Creek who's at loose ends for the evening. And who, regretting that he's missed too many of his own family parties, jumped on the chance to help celebrate Jed's great-grandson's birthday." He smiled. "Nobody will blink an eye at that, since every word is true."

To his surprise, it was, right down to the added cover he'd tossed in about his family, something he'd have to think about another time.

The only thing he hadn't mentioned was his plans for after the party.

She seemed satisfied with his answer, judging by her small smile.

Over at the castle, the huge front door opened without so much as an ominous creak. A woman stood on the doorstep. Slim, late sixties, with silver shot dark hair and a gleaming smile, she held her arms wide for the little boy who barreled toward her.

"Nana! Nana!"

At the sound of her son's voice, Andi turned and waved, then looked back at him. "All right." She hiked the diaper bag up on her shoulder. "Let's get this show on the road."

For a long moment he froze, hearing the echo of his partner's voice.

He hoped like hell this undercover op would end on a better note than his previous one had.

ANDI SIPPED HER after-dinner cocktail and tried to fight off feelings of both desire and despair.

At that overly dramatic thought, she almost choked on her drink. But melodrama or not, she *was* struggling with heightened emotions.

Surreptitiously, she glanced over the rim of her cocktail glass at Mitch, who sat at his ease on one of Ginnie's many pale leather couches. He caught her glance—he never did miss much—and smiled at her.

Her heart gave an extra throb, reacting like that of a love-struck teenager. That was just her problem. Exactly her predicament. She and Mitch couldn't have a future together, but her yearning to relive the past—to finish what they'd started as teenagers—was overwhelming. Wasn't that one of the reasons she had agreed to let him come along on this trip?

"Trey seems happy with his gifts," Ginnie said.

Across the room, Grant's family had gathered as Trey and some of Grant's nieces and nephews played with her son's new toys.

Andi smiled at her mother-in-law. Despite the risk to her flowing cocktail dress, Ginnie held Missy in her lap, helping her guide a half-gummed teething biscuit to her mouth.

"Oh, he's thrilled," Andi assured her. "You know I'll need to take most of the toys with us tomorrow. He won't want to be parted from them."

Ginnie had always been a loving mother and grandmother as well as a gracious hostess. She had been both that morning when Andi had made the last-minute call just before they left for the airport. First, Ginnie had asked eagerly about Trey and Missy. Then as Mitch had so calmly reminded her outside the house, Ginnie had readily agreed to include Andi's family friend on her party guest list.

She winced thinking about the other call she had made. Or rather, the text message she had sent to her best friend. She had told Cara only that she had had a change in plans—nothing to worry about—and would be in touch within the week.

"It's so nice you were able to join us this evening," Ginnie said to Mitch.

"I'm very glad you were willing to have me," he replied.

Who *wouldn't* want to have Mitch Weston? She certainly did.

Andi stared down at her glass. She ought to be ashamed of herself for a thought like that. Considering she sat here in her mother-in-law's house celebrating her son's birthday, she ought to be thinking instead of Grant. But she wasn't ashamed. She had put her life with Grant where it should be, in a special, treasured place never to be forgotten but one she would never be able to visit again.

If only she could get her in-laws to do the same.

She was happy to see the family again and had enjoyed dinner and birthday cake and Trey's excitement at his celebration, but she wished it were time for her to go.

Or did she?

She glanced at Mitch again.

In an upstairs bedroom, he had changed into dress clothes, a long-sleeved shirt with cuffs fastened with unadorned silver links and slacks as dark as his polished belt and shoes. Nothing flashy about him, nothing ostentatious. Nothing to show he was pretending to be someone he wasn't.

Well…someone he was, but tailored to match his role, one he carried off as if he'd been born to it. He had fit in with the Price family as well as he'd always fit with her own.

For all she knew, like Grant, Mitch spent a good part of his time doing undercover work, getting plenty of practice in taking on different roles for his job.

For all she knew, which was so little.

"Andi told me about the accident," he was saying. "I'm sorry for your loss."

She gripped her glass. He had to mean Grant. How had he managed to steer the conversation in that direction? And what had she missed?

"Thank you," Ginnie said quietly. "There's not a day that goes by that we don't think of him. I love seeing Trey here again. He reminds me so much of Grant at that age." She brushed her chin against Missy's curls.

Andi's eyes blurred.

Mitch nodded. "As I said, I don't get back to Cowboy Creek as often as I like, but I know her granddad is having the time of his life with the kids around."

Andi blinked and took a breath. Where was he headed now? Was she wrong to feel suspicious? "We'll be back here in Arizona again soon."

He laughed, but looked at Ginnie. "And I know Jed won't be happy to learn that. You know," he went on, "they're doing some reconstruction at the hotel and opening up the banquet hall again."

She wasn't wrong at all. He was fishing for details, trying to learn things he hadn't heard from her. Trying to *get* information from Ginnie by *giving* her information.

"I hear Andi's got a job there waiting," he said, "any time she wants to take it."

She started, almost spilling her drink. "I've told Grandpa thanks but no thanks," she informed him. "I've got a job in Scottsdale." She turned to her mother-in-law. "Ginnie, I think we'll say goodbye. I know you want to spend time with the kids before they go to bed. Should I clean my daughter up and get her into some fresh pajamas?"

"No, you shall not." Laughing, Ginnie hugged Missy.

"I refuse to miss any part of being a nana, including changing messy babies."

Andi's heart sank. She had tried to be strong for the kids and for Ginnie's benefit, too. She didn't deliberately keep them apart—or she hadn't until she'd made the decision to go to Cowboy Creek. But grabbing overtime every chance she could meant her free time was limited. Ginnie knew that, yet her mother-in-law often gently hinted she didn't see enough of the kids.

She set her glass on the cocktail table and reached for her purse.

Maybe she was reading too much into too little with Ginnie tonight.

Maybe she was wrong to wonder if Mitch had played a role with her, too, making it so easy for her to agree to this time alone. Most of all, maybe she was wrong to believe he'd given his word that they would talk only as a way of getting information she had been so reluctant to share.

BY THE TIME they left Andi's mother-in-law's house, it was full dark. It was also a typical December night in Arizona, dry and clear and a few shades warmer than at home in Cowboy Creek.

Mitch left the windows open as he drove through the neighborhood of widely spaced homes fully decked out for the holidays. Eventually their travels took them toward the outskirts of Scottsdale.

Neither of them had spoken much since they'd left the house. The silence felt companionable to him, but they had come here for a number of reasons, most of all, to talk. To give him the chance to help her.

"Want to go for a nightcap before we find our room?" he asked.

"Yes. There's a restaurant and bar not far from the hotel." As she had on their way to Ginnie's, she gave him concise directions.

"Trey did have a ball tonight, didn't he?" he asked.

"Yes. Ginnie spoils him, and so does the rest of the family."

"Looks like nobody's hurting for it."

"What does that mean?"

He looked at her in the flickering light from oncoming headlamps. "It means it looks like they can afford to buy your kid a toy or two."

"Oh. Yes, they can."

Silence again. By the time they'd gotten to the restaurant she'd mentioned, he'd had enough of the quiet. He parked the rental at the far end of the lot, just outside a pool of light from the streetlamp. When he turned off the ignition, she reached for her door handle.

He placed a hand on her arm. Her skin cooled his palm. "Was it cold for you with the windows down?"

"A little. But it felt good."

He slid his hand down to her wrist, trying to warm her. "You feel good."

"Mitch."

She shifted as if planning to back off. He slid his fingers down to twine with hers, loosely, letting her know she could pull away any time she wanted to. Looked as though she didn't want to, as her hand stayed in his. He swallowed a sigh of relief. "What is it? Having those second thoughts now? Is that what's got you uncomfortable?"

"No, that's not it. Not all of it." She stared through the windshield at the restaurant, a square, squat, fake-adobe building not unlike the Cantina. After a minute, she turned to him. Her eyes glinted in the dark. "Why were you talking to Ginnie about Grant?"

He shrugged. "Paying my respects to a woman who lost her son."

"That's it?"

"Yeah. Why should there be any other reason?"

"I don't know. Why did you bring up the Hitching Post and all that about my having a job there?"

"Because you do." He rubbed his thumb across her knuckles. "You know Jed would keep you on the ranch in a heartbeat if he could."

"You shouldn't have said anything to Ginnie. You don't know anything about my relationship with her."

"Because you won't say anything to me about it. But you can now." He turned in his seat, being careful of his knee near the steering column, and reached across with his free hand to tuck a strand of her hair behind her ear. "That's what we came here for, isn't it? To talk."

"In a *parking lot*?"

The astonishment in her voice made him laugh. "Yeah, you're right. We came here to talk—and for more than that, and we both know it. But not in a parking lot. Now we're here, though, no sense missing out on an experience we've never had together."

He let his fingers slide down another strand of her hair, let his knuckles brush the front of her sky blue shirt. The deep breath making that shirt rise and fall, the touch of her breast against his hand—both sent a hair-trigger response through him. His fingers tightened reflexively around hers. He had no idea what drove her, but she gripped his hand in return.

Swallowing a groan, he leaned down to plant his mouth on hers. She tasted good. Very good. But after traveling all this way, waiting all this time, wanting her from the minute he'd seen her standing in the barn doorway years ago, he refused to settle for a taste. He slid forward just as she inched toward him, enough to bring them together. Not full frontal contact, but satisfying enough to pull a few more triggers.

*Damn*, if he didn't have the raging hormones of a teenager right now. He'd summon the matching stamina, too, because he planned on making this a long night.

# Chapter Eleven

Andi slid onto her side of the restaurant booth and put her bag on the seat beside her.

"All fixed up?" Mitch said teasingly. "Let me see."

She laughed as she swatted his hand away from her face. "I'm fine. But my lips may never go back to normal size."

"You should thank me, then. You won't need any of those injections women get to plump theirs up."

"Are you saying I needed them *before*—"

"Before we nearly got arrested for indecent exposure?"

*"Mitch!"* They sat in a corner booth of the restaurant, Mitch with his back to the wall. She glanced at the table closest to them and beyond that at the row of stools at the bar. No one seemed to be listening, but she leaned forward, anyway, to set the record straight.

Yes, they'd gotten carried away in the car, and yes, Mitch had gotten her blouse unbuttoned and her bra unhooked, and yes, she had loved every minute. Every touch. But that was as far as they'd gone. "We did *not* get arrested. We didn't even come close."

"True. Where *is* the law in this town, anyway? Asleep at the wheel?" He smiled. "We sure weren't. Although I have to admit to a crick in my hip from maneuvering around the steering column."

She laughed. "Stop. Please."

He did stop, probably only because the waitress came up to their booth. After she had left with their order, he reached across the tabletop and linked his fingers with hers, the way he had in the car.

"All right, then. Let's talk."

Instinctively, she began to pull away. He didn't move. Of course, he wouldn't argue. The decision to back off would be hers.

Those words sounded so final…so familiar… The day she had met him near the corral, to shield herself, she had made her awful declaration about choosing to walk away. Years ago, her choice or not, she had walked away and left, too. And she had never reached out to him again.

Now she tightened her grip on his fingers.

Recalling the thoughts she'd had about him at Ginnie's made her feel guiltier than ever.

They sat there just holding hands until the waitress arrived with their drinks, accompanied by catcalls from a couple of men over near the bar. Mitch glanced in that direction, then focused on her again.

She took a sip of her drink. A Virgin Mary this time. No more after-dinner cocktails. She wanted to have a clear head, although to tell the truth, she still felt a little light-headed—in the most wonderful kind of way— from their session in the front seat of the car. Her first time making out in a parking lot. With the first boy she had ever loved.

She hoped this would be a night of many firsts.

The thought of what he might start in their room left her hot all over. She would let him make the first move there. But here… Maybe if she opened up about her past, he would follow and tell her about his.

"My relationship with my mother-in-law," she said

slowly. "You wanted to know. She's always been so good to me, even when I first met her. She could never take my own mother's place, but really, the timing between when my mother died and I met Grant was so close, Ginnie just naturally—eventually—became like a second mother to me." She paused, then added, "With Grant, the timing for everything was so close."

"You mean kids?"

"No." She shook her head. "We were already married before I got pregnant with Trey. With the timing, I meant Grant and I got married very soon after we met. The proverbial whirlwind courtship, a short engagement and then the baby surprise while we were still newlyweds. We were so happy about Trey. And everything...everything helped so much to take my mind off my mom, too."

She took a quick sip of her drink to ease her dry throat. "We were still in college when we met and got married, but I quit school before graduation because I was already pregnant by then. It was a high-risk pregnancy, and I was sick for the first two trimesters, then on bed rest for the third."

Mitch took her hand again and squeezed her fingers gently. She nodded in thanks for his silent sympathy. She could have stopped talking, could have turned the focus of the conversation to him, but she wanted to go on. To tell him everything.

"My father-in-law passed away not too long after we were married. Ginnie was alone in that big house and encouraged us to move in with her. We did, for a while. And we stayed close, buying a house in Fountain Hills, which is why I didn't move away right after...after Grant was killed."

He sandwiched her hand between his. She could read

the questions in his eyes, but he didn't ask them. His restraint made it easier for her to go on.

"Everyone, including Grant's family, believed his job involved selling high-end computer systems to customers all over the world, which is why he traveled so much. That's what we wanted them all to think."

Across the room, raucous shouts rose over the rest of the voices in the room.

He looked that way again. His momentary distraction and the noise gave her the chance to take a deep breath and let it out in a gust of air.

She was taking a chance now with Mitch. Taking a risk. But she trusted him.

When he looked back, she said, "Very few people know this. Grant was with the CIA."

His fingers pressed hers tightly for a moment. "On an op when he was killed?"

She swallowed hard. "Yes. I was pregnant with Missy. He never got to see her." Her voice broke. "Never even got to see her ultrasound."

"I'm sorry."

After another deep breath, she nodded in acknowledgment again. "I've come to terms with losing him, Mitch. I loved Grant, but I accept that he's gone. Only, sometimes…like remembering he never saw Missy, and knowing he missed Trey's birthday party, and realizing he won't ever share a Christmas with the kids…" Her voice broke. She forced herself to continue. "Times like those still hit me out of the blue."

"That's understandable." His voice sounded gruff, gravelly. But his hands around hers were gentle, his thumb stroking hers a tender caress.

She sighed. "You know, my mom was there for most

of my life—and for all of my childhood and teen years. But Trey and Missy won't ever know their daddy."

"That's not true. They *will* know him. Through pictures and conversations and your memories." His eyes were dark and shining. He leaned forward and said earnestly, "People die, Andi, but that doesn't mean they're forgotten. You won't let that happen. Neither will Ginnie."

His compassion helped ease her tension at telling this story so few people knew. At the same time, seeing how much he cared raised feelings she couldn't...wouldn't... deny. Feelings he deserved to know.

"Mitch, I—"

A loud crash from the other side of the room startled her into silence. They both turned to look just as a man sprawled on the floor beside a toppled bar stool scrambled to his feet with both arms swinging. A second man spun him around, pinning his hands behind his back. From an adjacent bar stool, a restaurant patron threw a punch at the attacker. Yet another man grabbed the patron and put him in a similar armlock, but his captive quickly bent at the waist and lifted him from the floor.

Mitch rose from his seat.

"Mitch—no!" A sudden flash of him in danger made her grab his wrist. She'd lost her husband. She couldn't lose Mitch, too.

"I'm just going to check things out."

"No!" Knowing she was overreacting, she took a quick calming breath. "Why do you need to get involved? Whatever's going on doesn't concern us."

"Those guys over there need a hand."

So much for just checking things out. "You could get hurt again. Think about your knee."

Mitch loosened her hold on his arm and lightly pressed

her hand flat beneath his on the tabletop. "I can't be a bystander, Andi. This is what I do."

He kissed her forehead, then was gone.

"I DON'T UNDERSTAND."

Mitch didn't need to hear Andi's words. In the halo of light from the lamp nearest their rental car, he saw her confusion.

"Why do you need to go to the police station?"

"I told you," he said evenly, "to make a report."

"But what is there to say? All you did was walk outside with those guys for a few minutes and then come right back in to our booth."

No. That wasn't all he'd done.

His first look at the intoxicated pair at the bar had put his senses on alert. Not for danger or serious trouble at that point, just the usual scan for any signs indicating a rowdy conversation would become a drunken brawl.

A later glance had told him the situation could get far worse.

By the time the bar stool toppled, he had known the setup was much more complicated than it looked on the surface.

And when the apparent onlookers joined the fray, he had gone to lend assistance to a pair of his fellow officers.

"Come on," he said, "let's get inside." He held the passenger door of the rental open until she entered the car.

As he walked around to the driver's door, he thought of what they had done in this car just a short while ago. Then he locked the memory into a separate compartment in his mind and focused on what he would do now.

Once he'd left the key in the ignition, he turned to her. "I walked outside to talk to two of those guys," he clarified, "because they were undercover narcs involved in an op gone wrong." He tried not to wince as he said those all-too-familiar words.

She sucked in a breath. He waited. "You couldn't know they were cops," she said finally.

"I could. As soon as I saw them in action."

She shook her head, puzzled. "I still don't understand why you'd need to make a statement. You walked over there after everything had ended. You didn't *see* anything."

He took her hand and held it between his palms. "I did see."

She frowned. "You barely glanced over at the bar the entire time we were in there."

"Andi, I'm a well-trained cop." Her fingers twitched against his. "We're taught to register in a glance more than most people see after a long, steady look. Before the narcs arrived, I saw an exchange go down and a guy leave the bar. Could have been money that changed hands, could have been drugs, could have been the key to a bus station locker containing a murder weapon."

"And it could have been a business card."

"Yeah, that, too. But it wasn't. It was drugs."

"Then you could have been taking your life in your hands by going over there."

She sounded full of concern for him…

Or distraught over yet another situation hitting her out of the blue. A situation hitting too close to home and family.

He released her hand and cranked the car's engine. "Taking risks is part of the job."

Taking hits.

Taking bullets.

Taking lives.

"I told you," he said flatly, "this is what I do."

"WHAT DID YOU say to that?"

Startled, Andi wrapped her arms more tightly around her upraised knees and stared at Cara.

She had almost forgotten she was sitting on her best friend's couch wrapped in her best friend's afghan. It wasn't so much warmth as comfort she was seeking from the crocheted wool and from the cup of tea on the table in front of her and from explaining the events of the evening to Cara. The events that had finally, sadly proven to her how dedicated Mitch was to his job.

She'd had to volunteer *something* to justify her late text and even later appearance on Cara's doorstep. And once she had begun, the words had poured out, just like the water Cara was pouring to reheat her tea.

"There wasn't much I could say to him after that," she admitted. "I could tell his mind wasn't on our conversation. He wanted to get to the police station to fill out his report. So since it was on his way, I just asked him to drop me off at the hotel."

He seemed distracted yet reluctant to go, until she reminded him the sooner he left, the sooner he could return.

At the time, it had seemed the right thing to say.

Alone in the room, she had felt the walls closing in.

"And then I texted you," she told Cara, forcing a smile. "I'm just glad you were here and didn't decide to go into work tonight, after all."

"I wasn't about to give up a night off. But you know I looked forward to it a lot more when you were planning to stay."

"Sorry. I must seem like a Ping-Pong ball, bouncing back and forth with our plans."

Cara shook her head. "No, not a Ping-Pong ball so much. More like a woman who can't make up her mind. Are you going to regret this?" she asked softly.

"Spending the night here with you? How could I? You bought the cupcakes, didn't you?"

"*And* the ice cream."

Truthfully, she didn't want to think about cake or ice cream. They only reminded her about the party tonight and her conversation with Mitch at the Big Dipper. Maybe if she hadn't pushed for the *where* and *when* of their talk about what had happened in Los Angeles, she wouldn't be sitting here now.

As it turned out, she had done all the talking. And she might never hear Mitch's story.

"Andi, you know what I meant. You waited a long time for tonight."

Cara had known about her crush on Mitch from the beginning. Her first letter to Cara from Garland Ranch that summer had been filled with details about Grandpa's new stable hand.

"I don't know what I'll regret." She glanced away and sighed. "No, that's not true. I do know I'll wish I'd had tonight with Mitch."

She couldn't worry about regrets.

"Everything doesn't have to be over with him," Cara said, "just because your plans for this trip didn't work out."

"Yes, it does. I can't have a relationship with him. Missy and Trey have already lost one father to a dangerous career. I can't risk having them lose another one."

"Nothing may ever happen to Mitch."

"He's already been injured. And I told you what he said—this is what he does." Her chest tightened at the memory of how finally he'd said those words. "Seeing him in action tonight, and then later hearing how he had kept track of what was going on—while I didn't have a clue—just proved it to me. Mitch may be lucky and never get hurt again. But he's all cop, all the time, and he always will be."

Alone in the hotel room, she'd had to face that truth.

Now she tried to deny the truth she had been about to share with him at the restaurant.

Mitch's compassion had eased her tension the way nothing else could have. His understanding set off feelings she couldn't deny. Out in the parking lot, she had reacted like a crazy, hormone-driven teen, but no matter what she tried to tell herself, it wasn't adolescent lust pushing her to make out with him. It wasn't fond memories or unfulfilled dreams.

She loved Mitch, more now than she ever had. She loved that he helped at the Hitching Post without a word of complaint. Loved the way he talked with Trey and Robbie and included them in everything he did. Loved how he held her gently and kissed her till her head spun and, yes, how he never stopped trying to find out what worried her.

She loved everything about Mitch.

Just as she had begun to tell him, the fight had broken out, he had run into battle, and she had lost the chance to share her feelings.

But she had to be grateful for that fight. It had saved her from herself. Her feelings for Mitch had almost caused her to make one of the biggest mistakes of her life—putting her own desires ahead of her children's needs.

# Chapter Twelve

After a nod at the clerk, Mitch made his way through the hotel lobby.

He'd spent more time than he'd expected to at the station. First had come his official questioning, then an off-the-books session. Some officers wouldn't have opened up or taken the help, but the narcs he'd worked with tonight were a couple of good men who didn't mind an assist from an out-of-town cop.

After that, they'd stood around shooting the bull. But tonight, the usual lure of sharing war stories couldn't keep him from edging toward the door after only a few minutes.

His thoughts had been with Andi, and that's exactly where he wanted to be now.

A stay in a fleabag motel would have done him just fine, but no way would that have been right for her. He hoped while he'd been gone she had taken advantage of the hotel's amenities.

He hoped she was ready for an eventful night.

As he punched the elevator button for their floor, his hand shook. Fatigue, possibly. Eagerness, for sure. He spent the ride up envisioning her in a plush hotel towel and nothing else, smelling like fancy soap and looking like his long-ago dreams come true.

When he reached out with his key, he had no doubt what made his hand shake.

The door swung open silently. The room was spotless and spacious, with oversize Southwestern-style furniture and a king-size bed.

An empty bed. With the covers still tucked up around the pillows.

He thought of towels and soap and muscle-soothing hot water. His gaze went to the open doorway on the far side of the room, but though his mind had already registered the dark bathroom beyond it, his subconscious had also picked up something along the way. Something he'd have noted immediately if his cop sense hadn't been dulled by dreams of satisfying a few other senses.

A stiff paper rectangle sat propped up on the dresser. A sheet of notepaper, folded in half and turned the color of whipped butter by the glow from the adjacent lamp. At least she hadn't left him in the dark. So to speak.

He stared at the notepaper, considering.

If he hadn't spent so much time at the station tonight… if he hadn't heeded the feeling in his gut at the restaurant…if he hadn't insisted on coming along on this trip…

Hell.

If he hadn't let things ride years ago instead of finding out why Andi had gone away.

The reminder pushed him across the room to snatch up the note. His hand shook just as it had in the elevator and outside the door. Not from fatigue or eagerness or the need he had finally admitted to himself, but from dread.

His instincts were talking again, telling him history had come back to bite him. He looked down at the handwritten note. Simple. Short. Sweet. No greeting. No goodbye.

*I'll stay with a friend and pick up the kids tomorrow.*

History *had* repeated itself—with a twist. The girl he'd once loved, now his one-night lover, had left him.

He crumpled the note in his fist.

THE NEXT MORNING, Mitch dropped off the rental car and made his way to the departure gate.

He'd had to drive a ways, but he'd found a greasy spoon for breakfast to make up for the fancy hotel with the big, lonely bed. The sight of the oil slick on his platter didn't diminish his appetite. After twenty-four-hour stakeouts, he'd seen and eaten worse.

He probably should have waited to buy breakfast here at the airport. As he now saw, he could have spent time with more pleasant company than his own.

He slid his overnight bag beneath a plastic table with enough chairs attached to make a quad.

"Mitch! Look!" Trey exclaimed, grinning. He was playing with a couple of the toy ponies he'd gotten as birthday gifts. "Little horses, like Robbie's!"

He grinned back at the kid and reached across the tabletop to give him a high five. Then he looked over at Andi, who sat staring at the paper-wrapped sandwich in front of her.

"Is this seat taken?" Not waiting for a reply, he planted his rear in the seat beside hers. His left knee twinged from the punishing workout he'd put himself through that morning. A small twinge, and he'd felt no backlash from it till now. A good sign of progress.

Too bad he hadn't had such luck with Andi.

His right thigh brushed her leg, reminding him of all he had missed. "I see you made it here on time. No sleeping in after a night of girl talk?"

"Who said my friend was female?"

"Very funny." This time, his grin felt forced.

After that Dear John note of hers, this lighthearted exchange sounded unreal.

She was putting up a front for the sake of the kids, especially her son, who was old enough to pick up on their words along with tone and facial expressions. He didn't blame her for that. It was the same reason he hadn't pushed her for answers the second he'd taken his seat. That, and the fact that she would just refuse to reply, leaving him unsatisfied...again.

"Jed mentioned you'd initially planned to stay with your best friend, the kids' babysitter...Cara."

"Grandpa has a lot to answer for," she mumbled.

"He also has a lot of answers. Which is more than I can say." He lowered his voice. "You planning on telling me why you left me high and dry and damned frustrated last night?"

Silently, she focused on the sandwich in front of her. He had called it right. He would have to approach her from another angle. "We had use of the rental all day. I'd have gone with you to pick up the kids."

"That's okay. I wanted to spend some time with my mother-in-law."

"Didn't she miss me when you showed up alone?"

Her brows rose. "Why would she? You were just there for the party since you had time on your hands."

"Yeah. And I had a lot more of it later on." He shot a glance at Trey, who appeared zeroed in on the ponies. Still, he lowered his voice. "What happened?"

"We chatted while the kids ate breakfast, and then I called a taxi to bring us here."

"You know that's not what I meant."

Her chin went up the way it had that one day at the Hitching Post. Then, he couldn't tell defiance from determination from challenge. Now, he had a bad feeling she'd just given him a shot of all three.

"Last night was a mistake," she said quietly.

Fool that he was, he couldn't keep his pulse from jumping. "You mean leaving?"

"I mean considering it at all."

"Quite a change in tune, isn't it?"

She turned away to spoon something for Missy, baby food or applesauce maybe. He cared only because it took his mind off the conversation. But a split second later, his thoughts went where they were bound to go. To where they'd been all night. To what might have been.

In the time they had spent in that restaurant, she had told him what he'd wanted to know—what had her so worried. A story she had kept from so many people, but not him. She had trusted him with the truth. Then why had she run off?

"Would it have made a difference if I'd gone up to the room with you?"

He saw her chest rise, heard her breath catch. He felt his own breath lodge in his throat until she shook her head. "Not enough to make it matter in the long run, Mitch."

She had told him how much she had been devastated by her husband's death. Yet she had said she'd come to accept her loss, and he had seen the truth of that in her manner. In her eyes. Still, he felt certain she was holding something back, trying to handle it on her own. And despite the way she'd walked off on him, he still wanted to help her.

Maybe, no matter what she claimed, she hadn't gotten over her loss yet. He could understand that.

Or maybe he couldn't trust his instincts about her.

Maybe he'd never be able to depend on his instincts again.

LATER THAT DAY, Mitch found himself wandering toward Cowboy Creek's sheriff's office, something he had sworn he wouldn't make a habit.

But in all honesty, he needed the visit to distract himself from an image he couldn't erase from his mind. He kept seeing Andi and the kids in the airport taxi she'd insisted on hiring rather than let him drive them to the hotel.

*How would we explain that?* she had asked.

Even as he'd opened his mouth, she had added, *I don't want to have to tell another cover story, especially one involving the kids.*

That kicker kept him silent, and finally, he'd agreed to let her go.

The bad taste *that* phrase left in his mouth had him yanking open the office door.

"Well, look what the wind blew in," Paco said with a grin. "Ready for a cup?"

"I'll pass, thanks."

"Sheriff's in his office."

Nodding, he went past the desk to the door in the rear of the room. He hadn't expected to run into his dad until suppertime.

When he entered the office, Lyle glanced up from the spreadsheet he was perusing. His eyes over the rims of his half glasses were as clear and alert as ever, but his hair was mostly gray now.

"Coffee?" his dad asked.

"What, are you trying to give it away? Paco just offered, and I turned him down. I think I'll get a cup of the real stuff over at SugarPie's."

"Good thinking. Don't overdo it on the bakery goods, though. I hear we're eating early tonight." Lyle propped his crossed feet on the edge of the desk and sat back with his hands behind his head. The wooden captain's chair creaked in a handful of places.

"Sounds like my old bones cracking, doesn't it?"

"Not that I've ever heard." He took a seat in one of the visitor's chairs. "How's the arthritis?"

"Good days outweigh the bad. How's the knee?"

Mitch shifted and felt the reminder of too much exercise that morning. "Doing okay. The good days are adding up."

"Nice to hear. Mine are going in the opposite direction. I won't be sorry a few months from now when I turn in my badge."

He looked again at Lyle's graying hair. Retirement had to come for his dad sometime. He'd always known that. He just hadn't realized it would happen this soon. "You'll miss it."

"Well, sure. Just the way your granddad did when he left."

"Leaving his legacy behind him."

Lyle smiled. "Just as I'm doing, son."

Mitch swallowed hard. He propped his ankle on his good knee to take the strain off the bad one. To have an excuse not to look across the desk.

Both his dad and granddad had been proud to have another member of the family in law enforcement. When he had packed to leave for the job, they had each taken him aside. He'd gotten invaluable tips from two lifetimes of experience. And, above all, he'd gotten the advice to "go with your gut."

Advice that had served him well—until a poor judgment call left him wounded and his partner dead.

He tapped his knee brace and looked at his dad again. "You'll be missed."

"I'm sure I will, for a while. But someone will come

up the ranks to replace me, and later someone to replace him. That's part of a legacy, too, always having officers ready to protect and serve."

He nodded, knowing that as well as his dad did. He'd heard that call even before his dad and granddad had shared it with him years ago. It was what had made him want to follow in their footsteps.

"Of course," Lyle said, "with all that shifting around in the department, we could end up being shorthanded around here."

He nodded, but said nothing. First Jed, claiming a shortage of wranglers on the ranch, and now his dad, hinting at a similar situation in the department.

At least *some* folks wanted him around.

## Chapter Thirteen

Mitch escaped from the glaring afternoon sun into the dimmer interior of SugarPie's. At this time of day, the sandwich shop was nearly deserted, except for one lone white-haired diner.

Mitch couldn't have left if he'd wanted to. Jed Garland's eagle eyes had already spotted him, and Jed's hand was raised high, waving to the waitress.

"I just got here," Jed told him. "Paz and Tina are finishing up an order at the L-G." He gestured toward a chair. "Have a cup and help me kill some time."

Mitch took one of the pink-cushioned chairs opposite Jed.

"How was your trip?"

He froze. Just how much did the man know?

"Nancy said you had to go away overnight, too. How'd your knee hold up with the traveling?"

Slowly, he relaxed. "The trip was fine, and the knee's improving every day." He wished he could say the same about his interactions with Andi.

The waitress, Cole's sister Layne, came to take their order.

"And how are you doing, girl?" Jed asked, reaching for her hand.

She smiled. "Fine, Jed. Just tired, but that's not news lately."

"I'd think not. Between that little boy of yours and the new baby, I'd be worn-out, too. I told Tina to let you know we've got plenty of room at the Hitching Post if you need to come stay awhile."

"She did tell me, thanks." After a warm smile for Jed, she took their order for coffee and went back to the kitchen.

Jed turned to him. "Missed you at the hotel yesterday, Mitch. We're getting kinda used to seeing your face out there again."

He didn't know what Jed knew or surmised or would make up out of whole cloth about his absence. Thanks to his years working with the man, he did know for sure the heights Jed was capable of going to for his family. And the breadth of his concern for extended family such as Layne.

He'd always admired Jed's kindness to others.

He only hoped his efforts at the Hitching Post had paid back some of his old boss's many favors. Because his days of playing assistant were over. "I don't guess I'll be around as much out at the ranch."

Jed's white eyebrows shot up. "Why's that?"

"They can use a hand over at the sheriff's office temporarily, and since I've done about all I can do at the hotel, I told them I'd swing by."

"You'll be back to help with the Christmas tree?"

He'd forgotten about that. Jed sat frowning so intently, Mitch didn't have the heart to give him an outright no. He looked down at his coffee mug. "With that crew at the ranch, you'll have plenty of hands to set up the tree. And I'd be no good at the rest of it. I'd break more ornaments than I got hung."

"That's a tradition in the family," Jed said, chuckling. "And speaking of family, Andi and the kids are back home. We're having a party tonight for Trey. You're invited."

"Thanks, but my mom's going all out for supper." Not a word of lie there. She'd insisted on making a big meal to welcome him home after his overnight trip. Because he *had* skirted the truth about that, and because she'd gone to so much trouble, it would take a stronger man than he was to miss the meal.

But this man could get used to having a home-cooked supper every night. Too bad he didn't plan to stick around.

He wouldn't even consider moving back home.

Jed might succeed in getting Andi to stay in Cowboy Creek permanently, and how would he handle that? How could he risk seeing her but not being able to have her?

ANDI SET HER cell phone on the bed beside her and picked up her notebook again.

"Let me guess," Jane said. "You-know-who."

"Yes." She had had several texts from Sandra at the airport this morning, then another round this afternoon. She looked at her cousin, who sat at the desk in the suite checking place cards against Tina's printout. "I can understand the bride stressing out as the wedding gets closer, but having her make so many last-minute changes is hard on all of us."

"They wouldn't be, if you'd put your foot down and remind her a non-family-owned reception hall wouldn't provide this type of hand-holding."

"*You* should be the one in this position, Jane. I won't say I'm a pushover, but I do want the wedding to be what the bride wants it to be."

"Like yours was?"

"Yes." She smiled. Planning her wedding had been one of the happiest times of her life, right up there with the ceremony itself and the birth of her children.

"You're such a romantic," Jane teased. "A believer in true love, and a fan of happy endings."

Sadly, the first two didn't always lead to the last. "I'd say you were all of those yourself."

Jane laughed. "You're right. I guess it's why I went along with Grandpa's plans for the hotel in the first place. Besides wanting to help him, of course—which I know is why you're in this, too."

"Yes." Though Jane also knew her other reason for coming to Cowboy Creek, Andi didn't want to get into it again now. She picked up the notepad sitting beside her phone. A few weeks ago, she couldn't have realized what her decision to stay at the hotel would lead to. But along with being a hopeless romantic and wanting to help Jed achieve his dream, she had had the overwhelming need to get away. To put some space between her little family and her many in-laws.

That reason needed to say hidden. How could she share all her feelings with Jane—or anyone else? She would sound ungrateful...would *feel* ungrateful...for all her mother-in-law had done for her and the kids.

At the party last night, she had felt more guilt than ever about leaving town with Trey and Missy to come to Cowboy Creek in the first place.

Long afterward, as she had tried falling asleep at Cara's, she had felt guilty about the way she had left Mitch to spend the night alone.

"You haven't said much about the party," Jane said.

Startled by the connection to her own thoughts, Andi jumped, then stared down at the line she'd just slashed across the notebook. She imagined Mitch coming into the hotel room and finding that cold, emotionless note she had left for him. But she hadn't known what else to say.

"The party was great. Trey loved all his gifts, and I had to bring a huge carry-on home with us."

"So I heard. You should have let one of us pick you up at the airport instead of taking a taxi home."

"I didn't want to bother anyone to make that trip."

"Oh-h-h," Jane said, teasingly again, "and you didn't mind bothering Mitch?"

"He—" *Drove home alone.* Swallowing the words along with a sigh of relief at her catch, she said, "He didn't pick us up." He *had* offered several times this morning to drive them home, but she had preferred to be on her own with the kids.

"According to Grandpa, Mitch took you to the airport. I just found out this morning. You never mentioned that to me, either."

"It was a last-minute arrangement. Like Sandra with the additions to the seating chart."

"Yes, but much more fun. I'm glad you're giving the man a chance."

"I'm not!"

Jane's eyebrows shot up.

Andi flushed. But she had only spoken the truth. Besides, after their conversation at the airport this morning, she doubted she would ever see much of Mitch again.

JED STOOD SURVEYING the dining room, where Jane and Tina were busy transforming its "simple, Southwestern charm"—according to the new website Jane had put together—into something out of a science-fiction movie. Stars and planets and spaceships hung from every light fixture, and crepe-paper creatures climbed the walls.

"Looking fine," he said. Their guests might not like

the disruption to the dude ranch atmosphere, but nothing was too good for one of his great-grandkids.

"They do look great," Tina agreed. "Robbie will want the same thing for his next birthday. We'll leave them up for a day or so before we decorate for Christmas." She handed a balloon to Jane, who stood on a stepladder in the center of the room.

"Thanks." Jane tied the balloon to the light fixture above the family's table and reached for the next one. "You know, Grandpa, I was just talking to Andi."

"Yeah? And…?"

"I hate to say it, but I don't think this plan of ours is working."

He shot a look over his shoulder at the doorway. "Careful. She might come walking right in."

"No, it's okay, Abuelo," Tina said. "She's staying up in her room with Missy and the boys so Trey won't see the decorations before time."

He waited till Jane had climbed down from the ladder. "What's going on, then?"

"That's the problem. I don't think anything is." She gathered up the packaging from the balloons. "She's not talking to me. Yet. But I get the feeling things didn't go well on their trip to the airport."

He swallowed a smile. Though he hadn't shared the news with the girls, his idea to have Mitch see Andi off on her flight had paid off in more ways than even he had anticipated. And this afternoon at SugarPie's, the boy had looked downright exhausted from what had to be lack of sleep—which he figured meant a promising sign of progress.

Mitch had gotten a little gun-shy about returning to the ranch. That didn't worry him any. He knew the boy would do what he'd agreed to and help them with the Christmas tree.

"Andi hasn't said much to me, either," Tina said. "We tried chatting upstairs, but with the boys running around the room, we didn't get very far. And truthfully, I don't think she minded at all when I said I had to go down to help Abuela with supper."

"Something's got to give, if Andi won't," Jane said.

Tina nodded. "I never thought I'd say this, but we may need to do something drastic."

"Hold off a bit on that," he said.

Both girls stared at him.

"Oh, don't you worry," he assured them. "Your old granddaddy's got a few tricks up his sleeve yet."

He chuckled, liking the thought he could still surprise them. Taking Tina and Jane into his confidence had worked well for him. But there were some things a man just had to do on his own.

Nobody in Cowboy Creek would have a clue what else he had in store for Mitch and Andi.

"GREAT MEAL, MOM," Mitch said to Nancy.

He sat back in his chair in the dining room and looked at all the empty plates. The rest of their family had already left the house, and he and Laurie were the only two still sitting at the table with their parents.

"I'm glad you enjoyed it, Mitch. And that *you* won't have to eat warmed-up leftovers again, Lyle."

Considering his dad could rarely make it home at this hour, the early suppertime tonight was odd. On the other hand, it had been so long since Mitch had been around here on a regular basis, he wasn't sure of the family schedules anymore.

He had more of a handle on what went on with the

Garland family, who lived by the clock when it came to mealtimes for the Hitching Post's guests.

He wished he had more of a handle on what had gone through Andi's head yesterday. Last night. This morning. He could come up with all the reasons in the world why she had changed her mind about sharing his bed, but he would never know the right reasons if he didn't get the answers from her.

A chance he didn't plan to have, since he didn't intend to go near her again.

"What's on the menu for dessert?" he asked.

"Nothing, I'm afraid," Nancy said serenely.

Another surprise. In his day, the Weston family had never skipped dessert after their main meal. Obviously, his day around here had come and gone.

Nancy poked Lyle in the ribs.

"Oh, yeah," his dad said, slapping his stomach. "I've got to cut back on all those sweets."

Now, *that* was something he'd never heard before. In fact, Lyle always joked that he would never get a reputation as a lawman who liked his doughnuts—because he liked anything with sugar on or in it.

Mitch gave a mental shrug and turned to Nancy. "Well, if we're all done, I think you ought to sit and relax and let Laurie load up the dishwasher."

"Or *you* could do it," she said. "Couldn't he, Daddy?"

"I don't see why not. This is an equal opportunity household."

Mitch shook his head. "Next time you're around, kid, remind me to give up my right to free speech."

"Never mind." She gave him her best devious-little-sister smile. "I'll help you out this one time, if you'll help me."

"With what?"

"Giving me a ride to Garland Ranch for Trey's birthday party. I have a present for him. And you could get some dessert." Before he could respond, she had grabbed a few dishes and rushed to the kitchen.

"I think I'll help before it runs too late," Nancy said. "Jed told me they would wait on the cake until you got there."

"'You'?"

"Well…" Her smile looked almost as conniving as his sister's. "Laurie and whoever she got to take her to the party."

Frowning, he carefully reviewed the evidence.

Early dinner with his dad home, but no dessert.

Laurie dropping her request and running.

Laurie's and Nancy's smiles.

And, topping the list, Jed holding up his family's party.

All proof enough to him that *his* family had joined Jed Garland as coconspirators in one of those matchmaking schemes his mom had mentioned.

A scheme that appeared to involve *him*.

Seeing how Jed had encouraged him to drive Andi to the airport, he shouldn't have been surprised. Knowing his former boss's unwavering concern for family and for employees old and new, he should have figured out before now what Jed was up to.

Leading him into a trap. Tightening a noose around his neck. Attempting to rope him into the Garland clan the way he had Cole and Pete.

And all a complete waste of effort, as the overnight trip with Andi proved Jed's scheme wouldn't stand a chance.

## Chapter Fourteen

The dining room was filled and overflowing into the hallway. At the moment, people were mingling and carrying glasses of birthday punch. There would be enough seating for them all, but with so many guests, Andi regretted she hadn't suggested using the banquet hall just to give everyone a little more elbow room.

Most of the ranch hands who worked with the guests were in attendance, including Eddie. The poor kid kept looking toward the doorway as though judging how easily he could make a run for it.

She smiled sympathetically. He would be happier if Laurie were here. The thought made her think about Mitch. Pushing him out of her mind, she went over to Tina. "Where's our other cousin?"

"She and Pete had to run to town. They should be back here any minute."

"Okay. I'm going to fill up another pitcher of punch."

"Great. I'll make another pass with the appetizers."

Slipping through the doorway and between chatting guests, Andi made her way down the hall toward the lobby. Ahead of her, she heard the rumble of a man's deep voice and then female laughter. With luck, that was Jane and Pete.

Smiling, she rounded the corner into the lobby. When

she saw the couple crossing toward her from the front door, she nearly skidded to a halt.

Not Jane and Pete. Mitch and Laurie.

Laurie's bright smile almost rivaled the shiny ribbons on the gift she carried. "Hi, Andi! Has the party started?"

"It sure has." She forced a smile. "In the dining room. You know the way. And I think you'll find someone there who will be very happy to see you."

Laurie giggled and took off.

Andi couldn't have described anything about Laurie other than her smile and the beribboned box. But she took in every inch of Mitch, from his thick, wavy hair to his button-down blue shirt to the polished belt buckle and black biker boots. After a long moment, she realized she was staring—and probably giving him the wrong idea.

Still, she couldn't keep from meeting his eyes.

"Trey, I presume," he said.

"What?"

"The someone who will be happy to see Laurie."

"Oh. Yes, of course, Trey, too. But I meant Eddie."

He nodded. "I can understand that. In his shoes, I'd be just as glad. In my own shoes, I'm not complaining."

He moved forward.

She rested one palm on the flat, steady surface of the registration desk. As Mitch reached for her hand, she couldn't help wanting to link her fingers with his as they had done last night at the restaurant. The memory made her hesitate just long enough for him to brush her wrist with his fingertips before she moved her hand out of reach. "Mitch, don't."

"What? Don't touch? Don't stare, the way you just did? Don't darken your door again?" He smiled without humor. "I'll oblige you with the first two. As for the last, I'm invited to this party—sort of, since I was Laurie's ride."

"It's down the hall."

He nodded. "Maybe we should wait a few minutes. With the expression you're wearing, it's going to be obvious you're not in a party mood. Look, let's just forget last night and move on."

She flinched. Hadn't she been telling herself that, trying to do that with so many things for so long? She hadn't known it would include moving on from Mitch again. "That's a good idea," she agreed. "You go your way, I'll go mine. I'm headed to the kitchen."

"That won't help matters. Walking around each other's as much a dead giveaway as your expression. Act normal."

"Normal?"

"Yeah. Smile."

Rolling her eyes, she forced her lips to curve.

"There you go. Now hold that, no matter what. No matter if someone surprises you." He reached out again, putting his hand over hers, warming her skin. "No matter if someone attempts to catch you off guard." He slid his hand along her forearm, sending a wave of heat through her entire body.

"What is this," she asked, trying to keep her voice from shaking, "a lesson you learned in the police academy?"

"Exactly. If you don't want to blow your cover, don't let anything throw you."

He moved a step nearer. How could she find him closer than she wanted and yet still too far away?

The front door swung open. This time, for certain, she recognized Jane's husky laugh.

Quickly, she stepped away from Mitch and pasted her

act-normal smile on her face—just in time to watch her mother-in-law enter the lobby.

THE PARTY WAS winding down. Trey had torn open his gifts. Tina was topping off the guests' glasses with the last of the punch. The cake platter sat empty but for a few crumbs and a smudge of frosting.

Jed, in his usual place at the head of the long dining room table, had insisted on seating the guests earlier. Odd for a kid's birthday party, at least in Mitch's opinion. Heck, he didn't care. He had made the first cut and wound up sitting next to Andi.

Now he shifted his chair closer to hers, trying to lend her moral support without a word or a touch.

She would never make it on an undercover op. In the lobby, in the space of an instant, he had seen her expression go from cardboard happiness to stunned surprise to genuine delight. She had added that delight to her voice when she'd greeted her mother-in-law. But he'd spent too much time watching faces and listening to voices not to pick up a disconnect.

He was tuning in to another one now, from the head of the long dining room table.

"I brought along the rest of Trey's gifts from last night," Ginnie was saying. She laughed. "But I can see they won't be missed."

"He was as happy to see you as the gifts," Jed said. "We're glad you've come to the party, too."

"Very glad." Andi smiled.

In the lobby, Trey's grandma had given him a smile, too, and a big hello, but nothing beyond that. Nothing to indicate they'd sat down to dinner together in her home less than twenty-four hours earlier. It seemed almost as if she didn't want folks to know they had already met.

There were disconnects and undercurrents and events going on around here that he couldn't figure out. He'd swear they all revolved around Andi, and not only because he had every one of his senses hyper-focused on her.

To his mind, her mother-in-law's showing up unexpectedly was a hefty coincidence. And he didn't believe in coincidences.

Jed's taking the woman under his wing, so to speak, and ushering her to the seat right beside his might be nothing more than a host catering to one of his guests. Or it might be another of Jed's schemes.

Folks began to get up from their seats and mill around the room. Andi went over to talk with Tina.

From one corner, Cole lifted a beer in salute, and Mitch wandered that way, stopping only to snag a bottle from the ice bucket on the drinks table.

"I see you grabbed yourself one of the best seats in the house," Cole said with a grin.

He shrugged. "I sat where the man directed me."

"He sure planned that well." Pete laughed.

Mitch looked from him to Cole and back again. He recognized a setup when he saw one. They were about to spill the details of Jed's latest scheme. After Cole's speech about the benefits of marriage, he wouldn't put it past his own best friend to be in on the deal with Jed. Well, playing along was always a good way to get information. He spoke in a lowered tone under cover of the conversations around them. "What are you two talking about?"

The other men exchanged a glance. Obviously, they had planned some fun at his expense.

"Matchmaking," Pete said in a low voice.

*"What?"* He shook his head. "No way."

Pete laughed. "Believe what you want, buddy, but I'll

bet my Christmas bonus Grandpa Jed is fixing to get you hitched."

Mitch looked at Cole, who nodded emphatically. "He's unstoppable. The man got us, but good. First me, then Pete."

"And he didn't try to hide what he was doing?"

"Sure he did. At least, with me. I was able to head Pete off, just the way we're doing for you now. But he was too hardheaded to listen, and look where it got him. He and Jane are set to tie the knot soon, too." He shrugged. "If not for you being too tied up with the job these past few months to stay in touch, you would have known all this already."

If not for his undercover op, he'd have been here in Cowboy Creek, standing up for his best friend when he'd married Tina.

"All I've got to say," Cole added, "is that the boss has one granddaughter left, and trust me, he's itching to get her married off, too."

"Not to me. You two can put that idea right out of your minds. He knows I'm not his man."

He wasn't Andi's man, either. Through both her words and her actions, she had made that plain.

Fine by him. He didn't want a relationship with the woman, just the chance to help her.

FEELING AS IF he had a target pinned to his back, Mitch stood for a while longer with Pete and Cole.

He saw Andi and Tina round up their kids to get them to bed.

Despite the way he had shrugged off his buddies' ideas, he knew Cole and Pete were right. Jed saw him as a contender in his matchmaking stakes. He still had his suspicions about Cole's involvement. And though he couldn't be sure about Pete, he'd begun to have second thoughts about him, too. About everyone.

He wondered if he was the last person in Cowboy Creek to know.

Why hadn't he caught on before tonight to what the old man was up to? Were his instincts entirely shot to hell?

His skill at watching other people's backs had surely taken a beating. He didn't have great faith in his ability to watch his own.

A short while later, Tina came back alone.

Laurie and Eddie had drifted over to a love seat in the corner of the dining room, where they looked to be settled in for the night.

In another corner, Jed and Ginnie sat at a table for two. They had their heads together as if they were old friends, which, for all he knew, was exactly the case.

The rest of the family and guests all seemed good to hang on for a while.

He finished his conversation with Cole and Pete and left the room. As he climbed the stairs to the second floor of the hotel, he noted with satisfaction that his knee hadn't stiffened up a bit. Progress.

Now he hoped to make some headway with Andi.

He tapped his knuckles softly on the door, expecting that the kids would be asleep inside. Andi opened the door just as quietly.

She looked surprised to see him. She also looked resigned. "Why did I have the feeling I would see you again tonight?"

"Wishful thinking?"

She shook her head.

"I want to talk."

"I'll bet. But I can't stand out here in the hallway 'talking' with you."

"Let me in, then."

Her eyes narrowed.

"Come on, do you really think I'd try to pull a fast one with your kids in the room? All I want to do is talk." He smiled. "You owe me for not blowing your cover when your mother-in-law showed up."

He saw her wince.

"Look," he said, "I know something's wrong. Something more than just being surprised to find me here tonight. More than you had time to tell me last night. And I know it somehow involves your mother-in-law. What else? Something connected to Jed? To someone else in your family? Is that what brought you back here?"

"I came here for just the reason I told you, to help Grandpa get the bridal business up and running again."

"That's not all of it." Her distress only confirmed what his gut had already told him. She was hiding something. "Talk to me."

He could see her indecision, and his need to find out, to comfort her, to protect her from whatever was bothering her outweighed the thought of any more strain between them.

He smoothed a strand of her hair away from her face. He wanted to stroke the fine lines near her eyes, wanted to lean down and kiss her, but he flat-out refused to give in to the urge. That wasn't why he'd come upstairs to find her, and for once he was not going to lose sight of his goal. He tipped her chin up to get a look at her eyes. They seemed unfocused. "I don't like seeing you this upset."

"I'm not upset."

"The hell you're not," he said evenly, keeping his voice low. "Andi, I'm not going until you give me some answers."

Again, he waited. Why did she have to make helping her so darned hard?

Finally, she sighed. "The kids are asleep."

"We'll talk quietly."

She opened the door wide. He stepped inside without making a sound.

Trey was sprawled across a corner of the king-size bed. Missy lay asleep in a nearby crib.

When Andi took a seat on the small couch off to one side of the room, he joined her. "I know you didn't expect me here tonight," he said. "But why were you so surprised to see your mother-in-law?"

After a quick glance at the kids, she looked back at him for a long moment. Finally she said, "I didn't know she was coming to the party, either."

"She invited herself?"

"I don't know."

"You were all right at her house last night. Why are you so uptight now she's here? Maybe Jed or Tina invited her as a surprise for you and Trey."

"I don't know," she said again, looking away.

He rested his hand on her shoulder until she turned back to face him. "I'm not leaving," he reminded her. He couldn't condemn himself for that. If he didn't push, she wouldn't talk, and it looked as if talking was exactly what she needed.

"All right," she said finally. "You remember I told you about staying close to Grant's family after we were married."

He nodded. "I remember."

"And I'm still close. I love Ginnie. You met her— you know she's a wonderful woman, and she's fabulous with the kids."

"And…"

"And I…I almost told you this last night. But it makes me feel so disloyal even to have these feelings. I just… had to get away from her. From the entire family." She blinked rapidly a few times. "They won't let go of Grant. They won't move on. They won't…they talk *about* him when I'm around, but they don't talk *to* me. It's as if they think I can't hear. Or as if he's the one who's still living, and I'm the one who died." She swallowed hard.

He kept his hands by his sides, not wanting to do anything that would send her into silence again.

"You were right, Mitch. The kids and I— all of his family—will always have Grant in photos and stories and memories. I would never keep that from them, but I can't act like their father's not gone. And I can't—" Her voice broke.

"Can't what?"

She took a deep breath. "I can't tell Ginnie the rest. That Grant left me in financial trouble. It would break her heart to know he didn't provide for the kids."

He frowned. "He had no insurance?"

"He had some, through work. Not enough for our outstanding debts, as it turns out. He always said, why would a man under thirty be worried about life insurance?"

"But you have two kids."

"I know. He thought he had plenty of time to worry about it later. We both did. He's not the only one at fault. But I've lost our house. I told Ginnie I wanted to move to a smaller place, closer to Trey's preschool." Her eyes shimmered. "I'm not sharing this to get your sympathy or your pity, but so you see why I needed some distance from her. I don't want to make up stories. Or tell outright lies. But if she can't even accept the fact that Grant's dead, how would she deal with hearing all this? And more?"

"More?"

She raised her hands palm-up in a gesture of hopelessness. "I need to take care of my kids in my own way. The best way I can. I need to stand on my own. And I can't say that to Ginnie, either. She would think she was losing the kids. So when Grandpa asked me to help with this wedding, I jumped at the chance to come. To get some space. To give all of us a breather. And, hopefully, to give Ginnie and her family time to grieve and accept and move on, the way I have."

He wrapped his arm around her and held her against him, her head tucked beneath his chin. She felt right there, as though she was made to fit there. As though she was where she belonged.

He felt her breath brush his collarbone as she exhaled in a rush. When she shifted restlessly, he took his arm from her shoulders. He felt lucky—grateful—to be sitting beside her. Though their night away had already triggered his need to have her, she had refused to let him get even this close. But he wasn't about to take advantage of her distress to push her into anything she didn't want.

Still, *he* refused to walk away without doing something to protect her from any more hurt.

"Let me help." He linked his fingers with hers.

Her hand jerked, yet she didn't pull away. He'd take that as a good omen. "You don't want anything from me, Andi. At least take my help with this. If you want to move *on*, then you need something—or someone—to move *to*." Hadn't his shrink tried to get that into his head? He'd resisted the idea, but he would recommend it to anyone if only it would convince Andi.

"Trust me," he said. "I know. You need something to let your mother-in-law know you're ready." It was his turn to take a deep breath. "Let's tell her we've gotten engaged."

# Chapter Fifteen

*Mitch had just proposed.*

Andi couldn't stop the wave of pleasure that washed through her. She couldn't deny her overwhelming yearning for that proposal to be true.

But she had no right to think about Mitch and marriage and pleasure all in the same breath, and she certainly had no intentions of going along with his crazy idea.

As if he'd read her mind, he released her hand and held his up in a pacifying gesture. "Hear me out. I'm talking about a temporary engagement. For a very limited time."

Her heart thudded in disappointment despite the cautions she'd just given herself. Despite the fact that, no matter how much she might wish for it, their engagement could never be real.

She couldn't consider his suggestion. But she had to know what he was thinking, how he could ever believe he could get her to go along with him.

Most of all, though she hated to admit it, she had to find out if his reasoning might not be as crazy as it seemed. "A fake engagement," she said carefully.

"Yes. You said you want your in-laws, especially your mother-in-law, to let you and the kids move on."

She nodded.

"You want your independence."

"Yes."

"And when all is said and done, you're doing this to protect your kids."

"Of course."

"Then let me help. Take what I'm offering, no strings attached."

She shook her head. There was nothing she could say. "You haven't convinced me."

He exhaled heavily. "Then, Andi," he said in a low tone, "consider this. Maybe they're protecting you."

She frowned. *"What?"*

"You said you've accepted that Grant's gone. But if you haven't told them that, if you don't talk about what happened, it may look as if you haven't come to terms with anything at all." He paused, then went on. "Maybe your in-laws are…walking on eggshells around you. Talking around you, not to you, because they know you won't take it in. Because they want to help you but don't know how."

"No."

"Think about it," he urged. "Maybe that's what Ginnie needs. For you to take the first step."

"But…an engagement? That's an enormous step. She wouldn't believe it."

"Yes, she would. After you'd asked to bring me to dinner at her house last night, and now after she's seen me here at Trey's party tonight, she'd believe it. And I think she'd be relieved you've made a move."

She shook her head again, not in denial this time but in confusion. She didn't want to accept what he was saying, but in some way his arguments made sense. What if he was right? What if *she* was the one holding everyone back?

"It would only be temporary," he reminded her. "We'll

play our roles, Ginnie will go back home, relieved, and after a few days, we can call things off."

"What about my family?" she asked.

He smiled. "We won't have trouble convincing them. You have to know Jed's already doing his best to bring the two of us together."

She couldn't hold back a soft groan. "I didn't know." She had been too wrapped up in Mitch this past week to notice much of anything. "But after his success with Tina and Jane, I should have realized."

"Right. And I've got a feeling Jed's mustering plenty of reinforcements. If we want to bring that to a halt, getting engaged will do it. Then, once we call off the engagement, they'll all know they gave it a good, hard try but will have to concede defeat."

She sighed. He had solutions at his fingertips, answers to ease her every concern, stories written in the space of seconds to fit any circumstance. What a wonderful undercover cop he must be.

But how could she go along with his plan?

She looked across the room at Trey, sleeping with his new space alien on the pillow beside him, then at Missy with her tiny hand fisted near her cheek.

What if, in the long run, she was making everything worse for them instead of better?

She looked sideways at Mitch. "A temporary engagement," she said slowly.

He nodded.

"Absolutely not for real?"

"That's correct."

"Betrothed *without* benefits."

"Copy that."

"I'm serious, Mitch." She kept her voice low, but stress

made her sound hoarse. "If you've come up with this idea just as a way to—"

"Don't say it. Don't even think it. I'm in this for you and the kids."

Blindsided, she sagged back against the couch. That little kicker had hit her like nothing else could. Except Mitch himself.

She took a deep breath and let it out slowly. "All right," she said. "You've sold me on the idea."

He'd convinced her his crazy plan would give her a way to show Grant's family that life could—and had to—go on after their loss. His plan would make her family back off, too.

If only she could stop thinking about her own crazy idea, one she was a fool even to consider. One she couldn't let go. The idea that this "temporary engagement" for "a limited time" might lead to something permanent.

"THE HOUSE IS locked up tight, and the family and hotel guests are all tucked in their beds." Jed turned to the fine-looking woman on the couch beside him. "I've been waiting all night to have you to myself. Now, let's get down to business."

Ginnie Price laughed. "I thought you'd never ask."

"That idea of mine of sending Mitch with Andi to the airport turned out to be pure gold, didn't it?"

"It certainly did."

He'd felt sure something would come of getting those two together in close confines. Nancy's phone call later that morning, reporting in about Mitch's sudden overnight trip, had confirmed his hunch. Ginnie's phone call today had come out of the blue but had him tickled pink.

He'd been just as tickled when she had agreed with him that Andi and Mitch made a perfect pair.

He wasn't quite as sure about her idea of coming out to the ranch, but he had to admit the birthday party for Trey gave her the perfect excuse.

"I was so surprised when Andi called," she said. "And I was very pleased to meet Mitch. We all had a lovely night. She didn't say a word about him when she came to pick up Missy and Trey this morning, though, and I didn't push her."

"You never let on we talked?"

"Of course not. You should have seen the surprise on their faces when I walked in tonight." She smiled. "I think I had them very confused, but as you and I discussed, I didn't acknowledge I'd spent the evening with Mitch yesterday."

"Good. Let's keep that up. I'll be the gung-ho grand-daddy, you be the voice of doubt. Then they won't suspect we're in cahoots."

She nodded. "Of course, I wanted the two of us to have a chance to speak to each other first."

"And to plan."

"And to plan. Although judging by the way Mitch disappeared not long after Andi went upstairs with the kids, it seems they might have plans of their own."

"Then, it can't hurt to help them along."

"No, it certainly can't. I'll try to get Andi alone for a chat tomorrow."

"I'll get Mitch out here again somehow, kicking and screaming, if need be."

She laughed. "Let's hope it doesn't come to that."

MITCH TUGGED ON his shirt collar, smoothing it into place. Then he ran his hand over his hair, smoothing that, too. He'd played plenty of roles over his years in the LAPD.

He shouldn't be this uncomfortable over posing as a love-struck fiancé in a bogus engagement.

"They ought to be here any minute," Andi said.

Last night, they had decided to break their news to Ginnie and Jed before they told the rest of the family. Andi had asked them both to meet her here in Jed's den this morning.

She sat quietly on the couch on the other side of the room, looking as cool and collected as if she made announcements like this every day of the week.

"I didn't bring you a ring," he told her.

That shattered her composure. She sat more upright and looked away. "A ring's not necessary. We can always say you wanted me to choose my own."

"Where's the romance in that?"

She stared at him. "There *is* no romance here, Mitch. You said this is all fake, remember?"

He took a seat beside her. "I remember. And you remember what else I said—when you're undercover, your best bet is to do what's normal in the circumstances." He reached for her hand and found it cold. She'd had him fooled with her unruffled facade. Maybe she would be better than he'd thought at handling a covert op. "Nervous?" he asked.

"Normal," she said. "Bride-to-be jitters are expected."

He laughed. "And grooms-to-be are very good at calming those jitters." With his free hand, he tucked a strand of hair behind her ear. Then he did what any normal groom-to-be would have done. He lifted her chin and leaned down.

He intended to give her a kiss as cool as her previous composure, as light as their conversation and as swift as it necessarily had to be, considering they were about to have company. But the first touch of her lips against his sent him straight to hot and heavy. And slow. Slow enough to notice he wasn't the only one doing the kissing.

It took them both a while to notice the sound of Jed clearing his throat to get their attention.

With a gasp, Andi tore herself away from him. When she rose, he did, too, slipping his arm around her to make sure she didn't go far.

Jed grinned, Ginnie looked at them with a puzzled expression, and Mitch suddenly wished Andi's impending announcement could be the real deal.

"Well," Jed said, "we're right on time for this meeting, but I'm guessing you two would rather put it off for a while."

"Yes," Andi said. "I mean, no, we don't need to postpone the meeting, and yes, you're on time. We have some news," she added brightly, "and we wanted to share it with you first. Mitch asked me… Mitch and I…" She laughed without a trace of nerves this time, with nothing but a show of bride-to-be happiness. "We're engaged."

Jed responded with a back slap that almost made Mitch stagger. Ginnie's hug was much more low-key, but whatever her thoughts, she put on a decent show.

Jed swept them out of his den and down the hall to the dining room, where the family had already assembled for breakfast.

At Andi's announcement, Cole grinned at Mitch, as if saying he had known all along his best friend didn't stand a chance of escaping matchmaker Jed.

Mitch gave his best groom-to-be grin.

"You two need to celebrate, big-time," Cole said.

"You need to celebrate in style," Tina agreed.

"Heck," Jed said, "you two need some privacy."

When the laughter at his pronouncement finally faded away, Ginnie said quietly, "Jed's right. I think a trip to

Santa Fe would be just the thing to…to give you some time to think about things. My treat."

"Oh, we couldn't—" Andi began.

"I think you should," Ginnie said stubbornly. "You're making a big decision here. You need to make sure—" She cut herself off, then she added, "I'll get on the phone after breakfast."

ALONE IN THE bridal suite a short while later, Andi sat at the desk and watched Jane, overcome with laugher, plop onto the bed.

"Wow. When I said you two should take a chance, I had no idea you'd come up with a scheme like this one."

"It was Mitch's idea," she blurted.

"Then that proves my point. He's still interested."

"It only proves he wants to help me out of a bad situation."

"Because…he's still interested."

"*Jane.* This is serious."

"So am I."

Feeling a sudden chill, Andi rubbed her arms. She didn't have the power to warm herself the way Mitch had with just a touch. And she was rapidly losing the will to keep thinking of this as just a farce. "I went along with him. I let him convince me. But I hadn't thought everything through."

"What's to think about?"

"For one thing, everybody in the family now believes we're really engaged."

"And all of Cowboy Creek will know in no time."

She stared. "What do you mean?"

"Tina and Paz plan to go into town to shop either today or tomorrow. If they make a stop for coffee…" Jane didn't need to finish the sentence.

Andi groaned. "Once the word hits SugarPie's, it will be all over town. What am I going to do?"

"You could get Tina aside and tell her the truth. You'd have to let Paz in on it, too. And Grandpa. But that's still no guarantee Sugar won't hear about it."

"This just gets worse." She slumped into the chair. "And then with Ginnie talking about a *trip…*"

"You'll have to tell Mitch's family, too. You might as well just stay engaged."

"Thanks." She glared. "I brought you up here to talk because I thought you might be able to help."

"I *am* helping. Don't you see how right this could be?"

"No. Not when it's all wrong."

"I don't know why—"

At the sound of footsteps in the hallway, Andi waved to cut Jane off. She reached for the notepad on the desk, hoping that whoever was approaching the suite would think she and Jane were busy working.

Her mother-in-law appeared in the doorway and gave them a small smile. *A smile.* Andi couldn't understand Ginnie's reactions. She had expected her to be upset, or tearful, or at the very least, resigned. Between Ginnie's odd insistence at first on their need to talk things over, now this tentative acceptance, and Mitch's suggestion that had started all this, she didn't know what to think of anything anymore.

"I have news," Ginnie said. "I know you didn't want to be away for long. I found an inn right in Santa Fe and arranged a one-night stay."

"Oh-h-h…" Andi couldn't catch her breath.

"That's great," Jane said. "Wait till Mitch hears. Right, Andi?"

"Oh-h, yes. But you shouldn't have." *Really* shouldn't have.

"If I hadn't, your grandfather would have."

Was that why she had gone along? To play the gracious mother-in-law bestowing gifts? But she had never acted that way before.

Confused, Andi nodded. "Thank you. I'm sure we'll love our stay. I'll see about it right after the wedding—"

"Oh, no," Ginnie said. "I was able to get a reservation for tomorrow night."

"EVERYTHING'S A MESS," Andi hissed to Mitch, her voice louder than she had anticipated in the empty banquet hall.

All morning, she and Jane and Tina had trained the Hitching Post's crew of waitresses who would serve at the wedding.

After lunch, the three of them had gone over new arrangements to accommodate the bride's revised seating chart and other changes. When Mitch appeared in the doorway, Jane and Tina had left.

This was the first time all day she and Mitch had had more than a few moments alone.

He came close, too close, and smoothed her hair as if she were a horse he was trying to calm. His touch had just the opposite effect, making her excited and bitterly disappointed at the same time.

Events were moving much too quickly, and in just a few hours, her determination to see this farce through had begun to buckle under the strain.

"Ginnie did make a reservation for us." Quickly, she explained. "We can't accept."

"We've got to, Andi. The whole point of this is to convince her you're making changes in your life."

"But we'd be taking her gift under false pretenses."

"You should have expected something like this."

"I didn't. I thought she would wish us well and then leave and that would be it until I could go back home after the holidays to talk with her. I didn't think beyond that point."

"This idea will work," he assured her, "if you can just calm down and see it through."

"I thought I could, but it seems too dishonest—it *is* too dishonest. You might be comfortable with all this role-playing, but I'm not."

"All the more reason for us to go to Santa Fe. It will give you a break."

"I can't leave tomorrow. I've got too much still to do for this wedding, and it's only a week away."

"Tina said you're ahead of schedule."

"Anything could come up between now and then."

"And if it does, at the rate you're going, you won't be in any shape to handle it."

He took her hand, the way he had this morning just before he'd kissed her. Warmth flowed through her from the memory, from the heat of his fingers against hers, from the sudden slow burn of desire.

Why was she arguing against their trip when all she wanted was to be with him?

The yearning triggered by that question alone told her what she didn't want to acknowledge. They might as well end this farce now, because a "temporary engagement" to Mitch for "a limited time" would never be enough for her. And no matter what she longed for, they couldn't have more than that.

"Look," he said, "I won't say anything to my family yet, and by the time we get back, this will all be over. But we've got to go through with it for now to convince Ginnie."

"I don't know. She seems to be accepting our news, but something doesn't feel right to me."

"Even more reason to keep up the pretense until she leaves. So we'll stay the night in Santa Fe, you'll get a break from the role-playing, and then once she's gone tomorrow, we'll come back home and tell your family the engagement is off."

"How will we explain to everyone else who might have found out?"

"We don't need to explain. It's none of their business."

"Mitch, you've been gone from Cowboy Creek way too long if you think we can get away with that."

He shrugged. "Then we'll say we had an argument and discovered we're incompatible."

"Due to irreconcilable differences?"

"That'll work. We'll admit our quick engagement was too quick, we didn't know enough about each other, and we've now realized it's better for us to go our separate ways."

She tried to ignore the tightness in her chest. He'd come up with that scenario so easily, tossing it out as though it was only another one of his many cover stories—which, she had to remind herself—was exactly what he meant it to be. "And when Ginnie finds out, then what?"

"Then you'll have made your point. Her reaction to our engagement shows she'll be ready to accept that."

She couldn't keep from worrying there was something wrong about Ginnie's apparent acceptance. Maybe she was only hiding her pain. Maybe she believed refusing to accept their "engagement" would put her grandchildren out of her reach.

But Ginnie had already booked the room, which meant they couldn't back out.

And once again, she couldn't fault Mitch's arguments. They made sense. This would prove she was ready to move on.

Except for the fact that she wasn't ready to move on from him.

## Chapter Sixteen

They arrived in Santa Fe in midmorning the next day, too soon after breakfast to have lunch and too early to check into their room. Mitch would have been happy to find an air-conditioned restaurant or bar and an even cooler drink, but Andi wanted to walk. She felt the need to unwind from the added stress of the past couple of days, he'd bet. She might also be wondering—as he was—how many beds they would find in the room they would share tonight. Sure, they had agreed to be "betrothed without benefits." But they hadn't let Ginnie in on the news, and she had made the reservation.

He tried not to think that far ahead.

They spent a few hours exploring the streets of Santa Fe and going in and out of shops to avoid the heat. Well, he wanted to avoid the heat. Andi went to window-shop.

He thought about her financial situation and knew it was on her mind, too, especially as they walked the aisles of a store filled with wood carvings. Twice, she looked back with regret at a small wooden donkey wearing a cockeyed sombrero.

A moment later, she exclaimed over—and bought— a couple of parrots with colorful tail feathers, claiming they'd look good in a niche in the dining room wall of the Hitching Post. "Tina gave me a budget for the hotel. These can go on the expenses."

In a shop filled with Southwestern pottery and kitchenware, she let herself go wild.

"For the banquet hall," she said, holding up napkins and a tablecloth in some rough material the color of dry earth.

"For a wedding?"

"Why not? Considering the dude ranch setting, some brides might prefer Southwestern style instead of our more traditional place settings. We... I mean, Grandpa and Tina and Jane can provide both." She'd corrected herself, as if making it clear her visit to Cowboy Creek was only temporary. "And they'll cater other events, too, not just weddings." Her eyes gleamed. "If I buy in bulk, maybe I can convince the owners to give me a good discount."

"Now you're talking. Tina will be proud."

She laughed. The sound made his heart thump extrahard. Her smile was the first genuinely carefree expression he'd seen on her face in days.

"And look at this!"

He looked. She held up a small brown rectangle with a large hole through the center. "What is it? A bracelet?"

"No, it's a napkin ring. Terra-cotta. *Perfect* for these napkins."

"Napkin rings and wooden parrots. You're not too hard to please, are you?"

"I think I am. I have very high standards."

"Oh, yeah?" That let him out. She fingered through the napkin rings, trying to find ones she could accept. Smiling, he shook his head. "You know, you really ought to stick around the Hitching Post. Jed could use your expertise."

"He's got Jane and Tina. He doesn't need me."

*I need you.*

He rubbed his chin and swallowed hard. The dryness of his throat made him wish they had stopped in for one of those cold drinks he'd wanted.

She turned back to the napkin rings, and he went back to watching her.

Wanting her.

But like a fool, he had promised her no strings attached to this engagement. And so he'd sworn to himself he wouldn't touch her. That he would sleep on the couch or on the floor or in the bathtub if he had to, but he wouldn't go near her—provided she even stayed in the room.

All those promises had seemed like good ideas...at the time.

"Looks like you're going to be here awhile," he said. "I'll probably cramp your style while you're chewing down the prices."

She laughed again, and his heart thumped in response.

He had to think for a moment to recall what he'd planned to say. "I'm going to take a walk."

"Okay. If I'm done first I'll wait outside for you."

"I won't be long." Just long enough to cool down some. Outside, it was still a balmy December in New Mexico, but the temperature couldn't come close to his own body heat right now.

He couldn't resist reaching up to touch her hair, to skim his fingers down her cheek and brush his thumb near the corner of her mouth, still curved from her smile.

He didn't bother to fight the urge to kiss her. Seeing how nervous she was whenever he got close, he wouldn't put it past her to walk away from him yet again tonight. To leave him alone in the room.

Or try to.

As teens, they'd had an attraction that wouldn't quit. They still had, and neither of them could deny it. He didn't know about Andi, but he wasn't about to give up on them now. Forget those promises he'd made. Tonight, if he had his way, they damned sure were going to have the one thing they had never shared.

He took his time, kissing her thoroughly, putting the seal on his silent vow.

WHEN MITCH HELD up the small pitcher of iced tea the waiter had left at their table, Andi nodded.

On the patio of the restaurant at their inn, a clay fireplace banished the December chill. They sat far from the streetlights in a corner filled with shadows. The darkness around them was broken by a tall vine-covered trellis threaded with small white lights. An ornate black metal candleholder with four squat candles illuminated their table.

Shadows danced against Mitch's shirt, highlighting every move he made. The white broadcloth made his hair look as black as midnight. She fought the urge to reach up to run her fingers through it.

They ate silently for a few minutes. She sipped her iced tea and toyed with the last few strands of cheese left from her Mexican lasagna.

She had hoped the time here would bring them closer, and it had. They had talked all afternoon. They had talked all this evening. Light and inconsequential conversation that still helped them to pick up where they had left off years ago, to reminisce about the past, to catch up on events they had missed in each other's lives.

No, they hadn't covered some of the most pressing topics, such as Mitch's injury and the answer to what they would do for the rest of the night. But she still had hopes.

"Did you enjoy your meal?" he asked.

"Yes." She had enjoyed the meal and the company and the sense of anticipation about what would happen next.

She had also enjoyed his kiss. In fact, she had spent a large part of the evening analyzing it—or rather, trying to guess what his unexpected act at the store that afternoon really meant.

So many contradictions.

It was perfectly appropriate for a newly engaged man to give his beloved a kiss that rocked her to her toes. But their engagement was a fake. His kiss was lingering enough to satisfy her completely, yet it made her crave more. And it came with the feeling of a promise she knew he would never make.

"Good food," he said, "but not as tasty as my mom's cooking. Or Paz's."

"Very true. Living alone in LA, you must miss home cooking."

He shrugged. "As often as I work double shifts or undercover, I'm eating on the run no matter what. But yeah, I miss that. I miss a lot of things." The flicker of candlelight reflected in his eyes made her breath catch. "Are you interested in any dessert?"

Was she interested…?

Now his every question, every word, every action seemed to hold a double meaning.

She could order dessert to postpone the pleasure of discovering whatever would happen next.

She could tell him the truth. It wasn't dessert she was interested in, but him.

She could take his question at face value and give him a straight answer.

"I think I'll pass," she said.

After he had signed their bill, he took her arm. Warmth from his hand tingled her skin. On their walk across the flagstone patio, the slight unevenness of the stones made her arm brush his side. The friction stimulated more heat.

"You feel like taking a walk?" he asked.

She felt like doing much more than that.

"A short one, if that's okay with you," she said politely. "And then I'd like to go up to the room and call home. It's too late for me to talk with Trey, but I can check in and see how the kids are doing."

"That sounds good." He opened the gate leading to the sidewalk.

The street was well lit, with merchants still open for business, trying to bring in customers in this last week before Christmas. She should have been back at the Hitching Post, helping with her own family's business. But she couldn't regret this time with Mitch.

In silence, they walked to the end of the block and turned back. When he released her arm, she immediately felt the evening chill and a wave of disappointment. A second later, she realized he had only wanted to step around her to walk on the outside, closer to the street. The chivalrous gesture made her smile to herself. When he took her arm again, as if he didn't want to let her go, the chill turned into a tremble of increasing anticipation.

If this kept up, she wouldn't be able to make the trip all the way to their room. She searched for something to calm herself.

"I know you're close to your family. Being away from them, you must miss out on a lot more than just home cooking." His shrug told her nothing. "Why did you ever leave Cowboy Creek to begin with?"

"You."

She gasped. Turning to look at him made her stumble. He reached out to prevent her from falling. The warmth and weight of his arm around her waist almost made her melt on the spot. For a second, his arm tightened, as if he wanted to pull her close. Instead, he released her and took a step back.

She stared at him. "You left home because of *me*?"

He nodded. "Once you were gone, it seemed like a good time for me to go, too."

A simple explanation. She had set an example for him, that was all. Why did she feel a twinge of disappointment?

Back at the inn, he escorted her into the reception area, where earlier the Southwestern decor made her think fondly of the Hitching Post. Now she thought of the last trip she had taken through a hotel lobby and her solitary ride on the elevator.

They went down a long hall papered in a floral pattern that made her feel they were walking down the aisle of the Hitching Post's chapel.

He unlocked the door to their room and ushered her inside. The bed, a king-size four-poster of knotty pine with black accents, dominated the room. The linens were bold turquoise, edged and shot through with silver. Other than the rest of the bedroom suite and a couple of chairs on either side of a small, square table, the bed was the only piece of furniture in the room. The only place they would have to sleep.

"If you don't mind," he said, just as politely as she had spoken earlier, "since you're going to be on the phone, I'll jump in the shower first."

"That's fine."

They were on their best behavior, acting like brand-new roommates rather than former sweethearts turned potential lovers. Maybe that bed would be only for sleeping, after all.

He grabbed his overnight bag and closed the bathroom door behind him. She waited for the sound of running water before taking a deep breath and sinking onto the foot of the bed. Showering—his, then hers—would put them so many steps closer to the rest of the night.

He had told her this engagement would be no strings attached. But they already had strings, past and present, tying them to each other.

They had missed what seemed like two lifetimes in between.

He had faced a tragedy in his life he wouldn't talk about.

She'd had a life of her own, a husband, children.

She had loved Grant, truly and completely. Nothing could ever change that.

But she had loved Mitch before then. And she loved him now.

The day had fulfilled her hopes of bringing them closer. Whether it was close enough for Mitch to trust her, she didn't know. Whether it offered enough for him to want her in his life, for him to decide she and her children meant more than anything to him, she didn't know, either.

Maybe they *would* be more than roommates. But maybe that would be only for tonight, and she would have only the memories of this one time to hold close to her heart.

THE INN HAD provided fluffy white toweling robes, his and hers. Mitch's still hung on the back of the door. She took the other robe and slipped into it.

He had come from the steamy bathroom with his hair

slicked wet and a pair of thin cotton sweats riding low on his hips. She had mumbled something and made her own trip to the shower.

Those low-riding sweats reminded her of the first time she had seen him in worn jeans, pitching hay in the barn. His hips were still slim, but the rest of him had bulked up and filled out.

She stared at the door, then closed her robe and made a secure bow of the long tie around her waist. She didn't have the nerve to leave the bathroom wearing only the nightgown she'd brought with her, but she knew this time, she would stay the night.

She had left Mitch on the ranch years ago, left him alone at their hotel in Scottsdale. Whatever happened, she wasn't leaving him now.

Whatever happened, she was going for her one-and-only time.

He had turned the covers of the bed down to the foot and lay half propped against a couple of the pillows. Cans of soda from the room's mini-refrigerator sat on the nightstands on either side of the bed, and a magazine she had seen on the table lay spread open on his lap.

She piled her pillows together.

"Before you get into bed," he said, "I left you something over on the table."

"You did?" A brown paper sack with the top rolled together sat in the center of the wooden square. "What is it?"

"Go find out."

She crossed the room and opened the sack. Smiling, she pulled out the wooden donkey she had seen in the shop that afternoon. He now wore a big red Christmas bow around his neck. "You shouldn't have."

"I had to. I saw you look back after we walked away."

"And when I was still in the kitchen shop, you went to get him?"

"Yeah."

She stared down at the donkey. "I'll bet he was sad I left him there."

"Very."

She looked again at Mitch. "I'm sorry about that. Truly sorry. And I'm so glad he's here now."

"I'm sure he is, too."

"Thank you."

He smiled. "My pleasure."

She set her gift on the nightstand and climbed onto the bed. As she propped up her pillows, the robe shifted. She eased it closed again, hoping he hadn't noticed. Not yet. She wanted him more than she ever had before. It was too soon for that, too.

He hadn't said another word. She took a breath and let it out slowly. "You were right that day by the corral, Mitch, when you said I'd want to have a memory of us. I do, to go along with all the other good memories we shared."

"Like that jackrabbit?"

"Oh. *Him*." She laughed, feeling her cheeks heat. One day toward dusk, when he had finished his work in the barn, they had slipped away. They had gone to "their" spot near the creek, where a couple of large, flat rocks made a perfect place for them to sit and talk. They had been doing just that when a stray rabbit bounded out of the underbrush near them, scaring her nearly half to death.

"Yeah, *him*," he agreed. "I don't know where we'd ever have gotten if he hadn't come along."

"You mean I have the jackrabbit to thank for our first kiss?"

"You sure do. Well, that and the fact you'd jumped straight into my arms."

Even the memory was enough to make her feel like an awkward teen again. Something she did *not* want to experience tonight. Struggling to think of what to say, she cleared her throat and looked away.

"There's a drink for you over there." He gestured to the can on the nightstand beside her. "I thought you might like a nightcap, compliments of the house. They've only got soda and iced tea here. For anything stronger, I can take a trip down to the restaurant again."

"You'd have to get dressed."

"I wouldn't mind, if you had a taste for something else."

"I *would* mind. And I *do* have a taste for something else."

She shifted on her pillows to face him.

He sat without moving a muscle, as if he wasn't sure what was going on or what he was supposed to do. His reaction made her think of her own indecision a moment ago. She smiled.

His gaze drifted from her face to the front of her robe, then back again. He shook his head. She realized his hesitation hadn't come from indecision but out of concern for her. "Whatever this is, Andi, it's not necessary. I told you this trip was just for show."

"Then show me."

"What?" he asked hoarsely. "How much I want you?"

She nodded.

He took the magazine from his lap and tossed it onto his nightstand.

She looked down at his thin cotton sweats. "I guess that proves your point."

He laughed, but shook his head again. "Are you sure?"

"Are you crazy? How much more obvious do I need to make this?"

"I don't know. But I don't guess I can expect another jackrabbit to come by and move things along." He reached across the bed for the tie at her waist and undid the bow. Her robe fell open. The sound of his sharp breath and the look in his blue eyes made her glad she had left her nightgown hanging on the bathroom door.

He slid his hand inside the robe, his rough thumb brushing her breast with just enough friction to make her own breath catch.

"You know how long I've waited for this," he said.

"As long as I have."

"But tomorrow—"

"Mitch." Through the robe, she touched his hand. "We're not talking about tomorrow. In fact, we don't need to talk at all tonight."

"That would be fine. But here's the thing." He smiled. "If I get started…not talking with you, I won't want to stop."

"Show me."

He moved closer and kissed her, long and hard, and then he showed her what she'd missed for all these years.

ANDI WOKE TO lamplight shining directly into her eyes. At first, they had been too busy to think of turning the lamp off. Later, they had drifted to sleep in its glow.

Mitch lay pressed against her back with the heavy warmth of his arm around her. When she stirred, he shifted away, easing her onto her back. Before she could move, he rose to one elbow and dipped his head, kissing her with a familiar thoroughness but more gently than he had all night. That gentleness made her want him all over again.

As if he'd read her mind, he kissed and caressed her until she was ready for him. And as they made love, his tenderness made this time seem bittersweet.

Afterward, she closed her suddenly damp eyes and turned onto her side. He moved to lie against her again, his hand curved around her lower belly. When he stroked her there, she felt an answering response even lower down.

"You do know it's still the middle of the night," he murmured.

She nodded. "I saw the clock."

"Restless?"

"I guess so. Or maybe just a mother's instinct, being always on the alert for noises that shouldn't be there."

"Yeah. Kind of like being a cop."

Just the words she needed to break her heart. "I'm sorry if I woke you. Have you been up for a while?"

"Give me a break, woman, I've been up quite a few times already." His laugh ruffled her hair. "And I'm having a great middle of the night. You can take that to court." She stiffened. His arm tightened just a bit, and she couldn't tell if it was in reaction to her movement or not. He kissed her bare shoulder. "I'm getting a good night's rest, too."

She forced a laugh. "Maybe that's not such a compliment."

"It's a darned good one." He rolled her onto her back again. "Actually, since coming back to Cowboy Creek, I've slept better than I have in…a long time."

"Getting out of the city is doing you good." In the lamplight, she saw his eyes narrow for a moment, then he gave her a smile that didn't seem any more natural than her laugh.

"It's not the city I needed to get away from." He sounded grim.

"I'm here if you want to talk about it."

"I'd rather talk about you. You're the one helping me sleep at night."

*"Me?"* Something else he attributed to her, just as he had made her departure his reason for leaving Cowboy Creek. "And how do I do that?" The question was out before she had thought about how teasing it might sound, but his thinned lips and tight jaw made her see this wasn't a light topic.

"Let's just say I'd rather dream about you than have nightmares any night. But we were talking about you." He brushed his thumb across her stomach. "You've got scars. From the kids."

"Yes." She half sat up to push her pillows behind her, then dragged the sheet up to her shoulders. "I told you I had trouble carrying Trey. Bed rest got me through the final trimester, but I wasn't able to deliver him naturally. Or Missy."

Through the sheet, he rested his hand on her stomach again. "You don't have to hide."

"I'm not. I had a chill." No…she'd had a chill last night. She had seen his scars for the first time. The glow from the bedside lamp had revealed a corrugated pink mass scoring the skin over and all around his knee. The sight had made her shiver. Now it made her frozen inside.

She hesitated, but couldn't go on. He had his secrets. She'd had hers.

She still had one. But not for long. She had one more truth to tell him that she couldn't keep to herself. "Tonight has been…wonderful."

He gave a low laugh. "As I said, I'm having a good time myself."

"Worth waiting for?"

"Without a doubt." He kissed her hand.

She reached up to touch his cheek. Dark stubble prickled her fingers. "I like you kissing me and touching me. But making love… When we were teens, I didn't know what I was missing."

"Me, either. But I thought about it a lot."

"I thought about it, too. I dreamed about you, especially after I went away. I loved you, Mitch. I still love you, even more now than I did then."

His eyes darkened. She could see his throat working hard, hear his swallow. After a long moment, he said, "Enough to take me as I am?"

When she said nothing, he rested her hand on his chest. She could feel his heart thumping against her palm.

Hadn't she known he would ask the one question she didn't want to answer? Closing her eyes, she turned her head away.

As he pressed her hand beneath his, she heard him sigh.

## Chapter Seventeen

They left Santa Fe even earlier than they had intended, and the ride home to Cowboy Creek felt longer than usual in the quiet. It gave Andi too much time to think about the man beside her and the question he had asked. The one she couldn't bear to answer.

Up ahead, she could see the final turnoff to the road leading to the Hitching Post. In just minutes, they would call off their engagement, as planned.

Admitting their romance couldn't be real, that she had no hope left for a chance with Mitch, made her feel empty inside. The feeling only confirmed what she had known from the minute she had seen him again. She had always loved him.

But now, she needed to walk away.

When they reached the hotel and he began to turn his truck toward the parking area, she said, "Just drop me off in front, please."

He kept driving. "I'm not letting you go in to break the news to your family on your own."

"It's all right—"

"Not by me, it isn't."

"I can handle it, Mitch."

"It was my idea that got you into this," he said stubbornly. "Besides, I'm going to have to face your family sometime. I might as well do it now." He parked the truck and took her overnight bag from the rear seat.

She hesitated, wanting to tell him again to go. To assure him he didn't need to take on her guilt. But he had already come around to open her door.

Sighing, she gathered up her collection from yesterday's shopping expedition. All the items she had bought for the reception hall…the parrots for the dining room… the gift he had given her —the wooden donkey with the sombrero and big red bow, a whimsical little reminder of a trip that hadn't lived up to its promise.

She would always regret this morning.

But she could never forget last night.

Her only bright spot in this very dark day was her son's greeting. When they went into the lobby, she saw him and Robbie in the sitting room. She set her bags on the registration desk.

The minute he spotted her, he broke into a huge grin and ran to throw his arms around her in a tight hug. "I missed you, Mommy!"

"I missed you, too." She kissed the top of his head, then gave Robbie a hug. "And Missy. Where is she?"

"At Rachel's house," Robbie said. "With Jane."

She didn't have to ask where Grandpa Jed might be. He rose from one of the couches in the sitting room and stood beaming at them. The boys ran back to where she could see they had spread a few of Trey's birthday toys on the floor. She followed, taking the rocker near the fireplace.

Mitch settled onto a couch across from Jed.

"Where's Tina?" Andi asked.

"She drove Paz to town for an order."

She swallowed a sigh of relief. That took care of the

rest of her family. For now. "And our guests are out at the corral for their riding lessons?"

"Yep." He was still standing, which puzzled her. In fact, he had started toward the door. "I'll just run up and tell your mother-in-law you're home."

She gasped. *Mother-in-law?*

Before she could question him, he was gone.

She turned to Mitch in dismay. "Oh, no. Ginnie was supposed to be on her way home this morning. Now what do we do?"

"We go to plan B," he said. "Until we find out what's going on, we keep everything status quo. But my gut's telling me we can forget the breakup idea until you talk to her after the holidays."

"But—"

"It's probably better to draw things out, anyway. When the time's right, we'll tell people we gave the relationship a good, honest try, and it just didn't work out. Till then, we can play the loving couple. "

"I can't." *Not after last night.*

He shrugged. "Take your pick, Andi," he said in a low, harsh tone. "Get everybody in an uproar just before the wedding and go right back where you started as far as your mother-in-law is concerned. Or wait till things settle down. You're lucky enough to have not one but two backup plans."

Now hearing nothing but bitterness, she swallowed hard. She couldn't understand why he would choose to continue the farce. But she knew she didn't have a choice.

ONCE MITCH LEFT, Andi fled upstairs for a while to be alone. To think.

Only a few minutes later, Jane tapped on the door, holding Missy in her arms.

It was the sight she needed to restore her. "Hey, sweetie. Let Mommy hold you." She reached for Missy and gave her a kiss.

"She needs a change," Jane said.

"You ought to be practicing those skills," she said with a shaky laugh as she pulled a diaper from the bag on the desk.

"I have other things on my mind," Jane plopped onto the edge of the bed. "Such as wondering what's the matter with you."

"There's nothing wrong with me."

"Right. That's why you look ready to bawl like a baby Missy's age any minute."

Andi finished diapering her daughter and cuddled her close.

What was wrong? The trip with Mitch. The finality of knowing they would never be together. Their arrival home to find they had to prolong their "engagement."

All that was too much for her. And Jane was too sharp-eyed not to notice.

"I missed my babies," she said honestly. "And we've still got so much to do to prep for the wedding." She *had* received several texts with new requests from the bride yesterday.

"I don't buy it," Jane said flatly. "Yes, of course, I know you missed the kids. I even believe you'd worry about Sandra. Who *did* happen to call this morning with an emergency since she couldn't reach you on your cell."

"I forgot to turn it on earlier," Andi said.

"I can imagine you were too busy."

Ignoring her cousin's smile, she said, "But that's almost a relief she called here. I can't imagine how she would feel if she couldn't get through to someone. What did she need?"

"Don't worry about that right now. Tina and I took care of it. And don't try to distract me. Andi, *nothing* should make you come home looking this upset after a trip with Mitch—especially considering the way you feel about him. Now, what's going on?"

She sighed. Reluctantly, she confessed the rest of the plans she and Mitch had made for continuing their act. "I just don't want to talk with Ginnie about Grant until the timing is better. She'll have so much to take in. And now, on top of that, I'll have to explain why Mitch and I pretended to be engaged. Once I'm back home again, I'll sit down with her. But until then, we're stuck in this fake engagement."

"I wish you luck with that one, cuz. It's not going to be easy."

"No, it isn't." Not easy having to be around Mitch, to play his beloved bride-to-be, to have him touch her, look into her eyes, say sweet nothings as if he really loved her… She took a deep breath but couldn't keep her voice from shaking. "We thought she'd be gone. She was *supposed* to be gone."

Her cousin's sudden interest in arranging the strands of her silver necklace against her shirt made Andi's stomach clench. She sank to the bed and stared at Jane, who still hadn't looked up. "All right," she asked, sure she didn't want to know, "now it's your turn. What's going on?"

"Grandpa didn't tell you?"

"No. *You* tell me."

This time, Jane sighed. "Grandpa invited Ginnie to stay for the open house."

MITCH'S DAY STARTED early the next morning, with a stop at the sheriff's office for coffee with Paco and a couple of the other deputies. He hung around long enough to keep from showing up at the Hitching Post at the crack of dawn. To delay having to face Andi. He felt sure she wouldn't be giving him the warm welcome a genuine fiancé could expect.

And he was right.

As arranged, he met Cole in the hotel lobby.

"You ready to play lumberjack?" Cole asked.

"Hell, no. I'm just along to keep you from getting lost."

Cole laughed.

In the hallway behind Cole, Mitch saw Andi round the corner from the direction of the dining room. She glanced toward them, then fled up the stairway. Mentally, he shrugged off her action. Cole hadn't heard her approach, and with none of her family around, they had no need to stay in character.

But the vision of her running away from him stayed in his mind all morning.

It was nearly noon when he and Cole returned to the hotel with the freshly cut Christmas tree. At that point, Mitch had thought he was done. He hadn't counted on Jed's roping him in to help Cole set up the tree in the sitting room. He hadn't counted on Tina and Jane's insistence that the tree be turned to every possible angle so they could choose the one they liked best.

Pete's daughter, Rachel, and the boys sat cross-legged on the floor, adding their two cents' worth.

Of course, none of them could agree.

Through all this, Andi sat on the couch, holding Missy in her lap and not saying much at all. She hadn't come near him, which must have made him look like a rejected suitor to anyone watching. And everyone was.

Maybe he should have gone along with her about ditching the engagement plan. Should have just walked away. But if he'd done that, he could never have forgiven himself. Andi wouldn't admit it, but she needed his help. For her sake, he had to go through with this farce.

Thinking of it like just another undercover op—a successful op—would get the job done.

When Tina appealed to Andi about the tree, she shook her head. "Oh, no, I'm staying out of this."

"What's that saying about too many cooks?" Mitch asked. The women promptly hushed him into silence.

From time to time, Trey would clap his hands and yell, "Bi-i-ig tree!"

Mitch couldn't hold back a grin...until the time he looked across the room and caught Andi staring at him. As soon as she saw he had noticed, she glanced away. Her cheeks turned pink. Good. She looked like a blushing bride-to-be.

After a last turn of the tree, and Tina and Jane's assurance the position was perfect, he went to take a seat beside Andi. From the corner of his eye, he saw her stiffen. *That* didn't fit her role. He wrapped his arm around her and leaned close. "Remember," he murmured, "do what's natural."

That went for them both, didn't it?

He brushed his cheek against hers and kissed those tiny lines near her eye.

Missy lifted her arms to him. He shook his head. "Not now, baby. After messing with that tree, my hands need a good washing."

Cole looked down at his hands. "So do mine."

"You both look like you could use an introduction to the shower," Jed said.

"Good idea," Cole agreed. "I'll use ours upstairs."

Tina nodded. "Mitch, Andi can show you to the one in the family wing. And Cole can lend you a clean shirt."

"No, that's fine. I can head home and get cleaned up there."

"Nothing doing," Jed said. "After lunch, we've got a busy afternoon scheduled. You don't think you can set that tree up and then leave the hard part to everyone else, do you?"

"Decorating, you mean? That's the fun part," Mitch corrected. "I always supervised my brothers and sisters when it came time to doing the tree at home." How many tree-trimming parties had he missed over the years? And who had taken his place since he'd left?

"I thought you told me you tend to drop ornaments," Jed said drily.

Mitch gave him a sheepish grin. When they had talked at SugarPie's, he felt sure the old man had seen right through that excuse.

"Mitch," Robbie said, "we gots cowboy boots to put on the tree! And cowboy hats!"

"Hats," Trey echoed, clapping again.

Mitch smiled. Suddenly, he had the urge to stay, no matter how Andi would feel about it. One way or another, he'd soften her up to the idea. And, again for her sake, he'd get her loosened up in front of her family. He'd consider it a badge of honor to coax a genuine smile out of her.

"I've got a change of clothes out in the truck," he said.

"Well, that's settled, then." Jed grinned. "We sure wouldn't want you to miss out on any family fun."

"We don't plan to miss a thing. Do we, Andi?" He glanced at her.

"Of course we don't. And we'll count on you and Cole to put all the decorations on the highest branches." She gave him a glowing smile. He tightened his arm around her.

He could see the effort she'd made, and the smile

looked damned good. Genuine and loving, as if she'd really meant it just for him.

This close, he'd wager only he could see that the sincerity didn't reach her eyes.

He ought to be angry she wasn't doing a better job of playing her role. He definitely was done with her pretending she didn't need him to play his. No problem—he had a few solutions for that.

Deliberately, he trailed his fingers down her back and curved his hand around her hip. The smile stayed in place, but he heard her sharp intake of breath.

*Yeah.* As he'd said to himself about her once before, he knew how to handle a challenge.

ANDI DIDN'T KNOW how she was going to make it through another minute of being around Mitch. She had had as much as she could take of seeing his smile, of hearing his laugh. He had done a lot of both during lunch in the dining room, then even more since they had spent the afternoon in the sitting room decorating the tree.

"Cole," he said now, "you call yourself a wrangler? I could've done a better job of roping and tying that garland to the tree, and I haven't worked this ranch in years."

He sat on the couch with Missy on his knee and the boys and Rachel close by on the floor near his feet. All afternoon, he had talked with them and teased them and treated them as if they were his own kids.

She'd had enough of keeping up pretenses in front of her family. But he continued playing his role. He had brought her into conversations, too, when she would rather have been quiet. He had taken every chance available to put his arm around her. He had smiled at her like a man in love.

It all made her heart hurt.

Her mother-in-law had left the hotel for a visit of her own to friends in Santa Fe. That provided a reprieve, but not a long one. She would be back in a couple of days.

And there was still her family to deal with. Other than Jane, she couldn't share the truth with the rest of them. She was having a hard enough time pretending everything was happy and normal. She couldn't drag them all into this farce, too.

She rose from her chair. "I'll bring some more punch." She was only halfway through the doorway into the lobby when laughter broke out behind her and she felt a hand on her arm. She turned to find Mitch smiling at her. Because he knew he had to. The thought left her misty-eyed.

He still held Missy, who had curled her fingers in his hair.

With his free hand, he pointed upward. She didn't need to look to know exactly what she would find. She stood directly beneath the sprig of mistletoe Jed had hung from the door frame.

"Oh, boy," Rachel said, laughing. "Grandpa Jed told me what that means."

She knew what it meant, too. But she couldn't stand here and kiss Mitch in front of all her family. She might be playing a role for them, but his mouth on hers would be all too real.

"I think I caught you," he murmured.

A long, long time ago.

"Yes," she said with an exaggerated sigh, "I think you did. Well, never let it be said I passed up a great opportunity." She smiled, leaned forward and kissed her daughter's cheek.

He scowled.

She laughed along with everyone else, then darted away and across the lobby.

"Hey, Mitch," Cole called, "who's the better wrangler now? At least I held on to that garland, which is more than you can say about your girl."

"We'll see about that."

She heard Mitch's boots thundering across the lobby's wooden floor. She was halfway down the hall to the kitchen when he caught up with her and swung her to face him.

"Hey, you forgot something."

"Oh, no, I didn't." She matched his teasing tone, saying the words loudly enough for those in the sitting room to hear. Then she lowered her voice. "We're alone now. You can drop the act."

"Who's acting?" he said huskily. "At Christmastime, nobody ignores the mistletoe and gets away with it."

"I didn't ignore it."

He grinned. "All right, then—nobody ignores *me*." Taking her by the hand, he led her the few feet to Jed's den and closed the door behind them. Then he turned and wrapped his arms around her.

Everywhere his body touched hers, she felt the heat, as if a string of Christmas lights draped between them had sparked to life. Those lights definitely twinkled brightly as he lowered his head to steal the kiss she had refused to give him. She wanted to refuse him now, but he had his mouth on hers and his fingers threaded through her hair, holding her close and steady, just the way she liked him to kiss her.

Just what she didn't need.

She pulled herself away and backed off, still feeling the tingle everywhere they had touched.

He ran his hand through his hair and looked as dismayed as she felt.

"Well," she said, exhaling heavily, "I don't think our agreement calls for kissing in private."

Mitch exhaled just as heavily and watched as Andi moved to lean against Jed's desk. She shook her head, making all that blond hair he'd just run his hands through tumble around her shoulders. His hands and his mouth and his body ached to get back to where they'd left off.

"I think we'd better call a halt to this playacting," she said. "I can't keep doing it anymore."

"We can take a break from it for a few days."

"Take a break? How is that going to work?"

"I could try not talking to you, the way you've done all day with me."

"So that's what this is all about?" She gestured between them. "Male pride? I wouldn't talk to you and then I wouldn't kiss you, and this is how you get your feelings across?"

"I don't do feelings. And *this is all about* what it's been all along. Helping you cut the cord to your in-laws."

She had the grace to blush. It did nothing to ease his irritation. "Look. I'll admit we do need a break. I'll find a reason to stay in town tomorrow, and then I'll be leaving for LA."

"Leaving?"

She sounded startled. He wished she sounded sad, then wished he hadn't had any reaction at all. "I've got a visit lined up with the surgeon who operated on my knee. If all goes well, I should be declared fit for duty again soon."

"I hope you get a good report."

Now he heard only politeness in her tone. He had known she wouldn't feel overjoyed at this news. The fact that he didn't mean more to her made him want to walk away without another word.

And still, he couldn't leave without trying to do what he could to help.

"I hope the report is good, too," he said seriously. "I've had some bad things happen on the job, Andi. Seen some bad things go down. They only reinforced what I've always known—there are no guarantees in life. That doesn't mean folks stop living. I don't think you get the point that life goes on."

"Of course I do. That's exactly what losing Grant taught me."

"No," he insisted. "I'm not talking about becoming independent—which is what you've claimed all along to want."

"Because it is. That's why we agreed to this fake engagement. So I could show Ginnie how I felt."

"No," he said again. "You told me that, most of all, you wanted to show your mother-in-law life goes on after a loss. Yet you're not willing to take your own advice and move on."

"But I am moving on."

"Yeah. As long as wherever you go, you're working with a safety net. That's not always going to happen, no matter how well you plan." He rubbed his jaw and sighed. "This trip to see the surgeon... You wanted to know what happened. The injury occurred at the same time I lost my partner in an op that got shot to hell. And it was my fault he died."

He had never stated the truth that plainly to anyone but himself. "I can't discuss an open case, and the details aren't important, anyway. What matters is, my partner on the op and I were undercover, working at a warehouse targeted for a raid.

"I'd had a bad feeling about the perps we were dealing with. And though my partner hadn't had his cover blown, he'd run into some trouble with them. He out-ranked me and had the bigger role in the op. The day the raid was scheduled, he wanted to stay in role and canvass the warehouse ahead of the team."

"If he was in charge, then how could what happened be your fault?"

"Because I didn't follow my instincts."

"He made the decision, you didn't. And you said he had seniority."

"Yeah. He pulled rank, and I gave in."

"I still don't see where you're at fault."

"I knew—I *knew*—he shouldn't go near that warehouse. And because I didn't stop him, because I didn't listen to my gut, he was caught in an ambush."

She closed her eyes, the way she had done at the inn. Her face turned pale.

This time, he was the one to look away. He didn't close his eyes. Experience had taught him he would see the scene too clearly. "By the time I got inside, he was dead and so was one of the perps. The other turned his sights on me. I managed to get off a couple of rounds, but my weapon was nothing against his AK. It blasted my knee—and that was the good news. It was the only thing that saved me. I landed flat on my ass just as our backup stormed in."

He looked at her and saw her eyes shimmering with tears. He had to get some distance before he could tell her the rest. He walked to a corner bookshelf, where he stood looking down at a photo of Jed and Paz and the Garland clan.

"They slaughtered my partner," he said, knowing he had to keep his voice low or he'd lose control altogether. "He was only a few years from a full pension and had a wife and three kids. They carried me out on a stretcher, but they took him away in a body bag. Because I didn't follow my damned gut."

From behind him, he heard her choke back a sob. His throat tightened. He looked down at the photo again and took a deep breath.

Then he turned back to Andi. He could see the horror in her tear-filled eyes.

"If ever a time could have come when I would debate handing in my shield, it would've been then. But even with all that—surgery and rehab and knowing I could have saved my partner if I'd done the right thing—even after all that, I'm still on the force. I told you, it's what I do. But it's more than that." He sighed.

"I know what you're looking for, Andi. And I know how you feel. But if you can't accept the work I do, there's nothing more I can say. Because for me, being a cop isn't just a job. It's who I am."

# Chapter Eighteen

In his surgeon's offices in LA, sitting half-undressed and freezing his butt off in an examining room, Mitch flipped through an outdated magazine, studied the anatomy charts on the wall and tried to guess the number of surgical gloves in a monster-size carton near the corner sink.

Anything to keep from thinking about his last conversation with Andi.

The doctor entered the office carrying a file folder. He usually looked like a blue-eyed basset hound who'd had his last bone stolen. Today, he appeared to have gotten a new treat.

"Good news, Doc?" he asked hopefully.

"The X-rays show improvement. Let's see how the rest measures up."

The man put him through his paces, checking range of motion, stability, flexibility and a list of other things. Mitch aced the tests, gave ratings of pain on a scale from one to ten, and earned another smile.

"You seem to be following the exercise program."

"Yeah." He thought of his night in Santa Fe with Andi and knew he probably had her to thank for some of these improvements.

He also realized he'd now have to accomplish any future progress on his own.

The doctor went over the list of modifications to the exercises, scribbled something on a form, then finally slapped the file folder closed. "Questions?"

"Any idea when I'm going back on duty?"

He knew his return would also depend on the shrink's report but felt sure he would ace that evaluation. He was more concerned now about questions he couldn't put into words. Mentally, he was back where he should be, but physically...

The man gave him his basset-hound smile. "As you know, the final decision regarding your status isn't up to me.

"At this rate," the surgeon went on, "I would anticipate seeing you back to full strength by your next appointment with me. But from this point, everything depends on you."

"And I'm nothing if not reliable."

He froze, waited, considered. A few weeks ago, he'd have had second thoughts after making that statement. Now, nothing. Except the knowledge it was true. "Don't worry, Doc. You can count on me."

The surgeon eyed him for a moment, then nodded. "Good. And I'm recommending your immediate return to desk duty."

He hadn't noticed he'd been holding his breath until he exhaled and felt ten tons of pressure leave his chest. He hadn't realized how much he'd had riding on this report.

Even as a kid, he had been athletic, and while he didn't expect or want to be star quarterback again, he wanted to do his job...now more than ever, since it seemed likely the job might be all he ever had.

AT THE STATION, he shook a lot of hands and received a lot of back slaps. He heard stories of ops that had ended in disaster and of cops who had recovered and moved on.

He had begun to believe he was past the worst of the memories...until he took a turn down the hall leading to the interrogation rooms and almost ran over a woman who stopped dead in her tracks in front of him. She looked at him through the familiar bright red–rimmed glasses that went with her bright red hair. She went by the familiar title of department shrink.

"Hello, Mitch."

"Janice." He nodded. "What brings you to my neighborhood?"

"I needed to discuss a few things with the chief. You haven't forgotten our appointment?"

"Wouldn't miss it." With luck this afternoon's meeting would be their last.

She peered down at her watch. "I could fit you in now if you'd rather not wait till later."

"At your office?"

"Why not right here?" She gestured to a couple of open doorways.

He didn't much go for the idea of meeting in an interrogation room, but the space was available, and he did want to get this over with.

After a quick word with the desk sergeant, he escorted Janice into a free room. She set her briefcase on the scarred tabletop and settled back in her chair.

He took the one opposite hers.

"How have you been sleeping?" she asked.

"Better. Much better. Like a baby, in fact." And it was true. As he had told Andi, she had helped him sleep. *I'd rather dream about you than have nightmares any night.* What he hadn't said was what an accomplishment that had been.

"How's the knee doing?" she asked.

"Great. I just got cleared for desk duty by the surgeon this morning."

"Ah. How does that make you feel?"

He'd learned to hate that question.

He set his jaw and stared at the blank white wall behind her for a moment before looking back. "We're closing in on our final session." He smiled to soften his words. "Shouldn't we be moving on? Aren't these meetings supposed to show progress on both sides?"

"Some of my clients seem to think so," she said drily. "What they sometimes don't want to acknowledge is that progress can mean taking a few steps backward. When we do that as a team, I can help them face reality. And that also often involves sharing their feelings."

He laughed. "Come on, Doc, I've told you before. I'm a guy. And a seasoned cop." Again, he thought of what he had told Andi. "I don't do feelings."

"Except at the appropriate times."

He narrowed his eyes. She might have gotten him into a claustrophobic interrogation room, but she wasn't trapping him in this conversation. "Such as?"

"When you're trying to get a suspect to crack, you play on their emotions."

"Well, yeah. Whatever works."

"If you're confronting someone holding victims at gun- or knifepoint, you talk them down."

"Sure. Basic negotiation."

"And when you have a friend upset about a problem, you help him think the situation through."

"Of course." He laughed shortly. "Okay. If you want to talk about dealing with reality, take a look at this scenario. A woman with two kids. Recently lost her husband. She thinks her in-laws are having trouble letting go. They don't want to believe he's dead, are trying to act like nothing happened, and—" Swearing silently, he cut himself off.

"And they don't want to talk about how that feels." She tugged on her glasses to eye him over the frame. "Like someone else I know."

How many times had she tried leading him down that road? *Not sleeping at night, having those nightmares, might be a sign you need to voice your feelings.*

As she stared him down, he sighed. "All right. You don't need to beat me over the head with it."

She laughed. "You know I would never do that. This woman is someone you know personally?"

*Intimately.* He shrugged and shoved his hands into his pockets. "We...went out when we were teenagers."

"You saw her again on your visit back home."

"Yeah. For the first time in a long time. Since we were teens, as a matter of fact."

"That must have brought back memories—"

"It sure did."

"—which are often based on feelings. And those feelings frequently hover just beneath the surface—or even come out into the open—when those memories are being shared."

He grimaced. "You got me there, Doc."

"I don't want to get you, Mitch. I want to help you. The way you want to help your friend." She smiled. "You could start by asking her—"

"I already know. She told me how she feels."

"Then maybe it's your turn."

"I did tell her. She doesn't want to listen, and I've got nothing more to say."

"Sounds like it's time for negotiation...if you want to see progress on both sides." When he didn't reply, she added, "Now we *are* close to the end of our sessions,

I'll ask you the same question I did in our first meeting. How do you feel you've been affected by the trauma you suffered?"

He shrugged. Drummed his fingers on the edge of the table. Looked away from those all-seeing eyes. "I'll have to get back to you on that one."

Again, he thought of Andi.

How could he expect something of her he couldn't manage to do himself?

IN THE DAYS Mitch was away, any time Andi found herself on her own, she couldn't help thinking of him. So she did her best to make sure she was never alone.

That wasn't as difficult as she had expected.

During preparations for the rehearsal dinner and wedding, she found a never-ending list of jobs to keep her mind on business.

Once the bridal party and wedding guests began arriving, she had even less time to brood. Her family, including Ginnie, had less time to question her about Mitch. They were all so busy entertaining the Hitching Post's guests.

Once in a while, she had to sidestep a comment about him. She managed that. What she couldn't bear was Trey's puzzled expression when he looked around a crowded room, then asked, "Where Mitch?"

It was only in her room at night, when she tossed and turned and watched her children sleep, that she stopped fighting her thoughts.

Mitch hadn't contacted her once. She mulled over everything they had said to each other since their last conversation, ran through every bittersweet moment of their one night together and wondered about the results of his doctor's appointment.

She thought of his accusation about not being willing to move on. She *had* moved on…except when it came to him.

Most of all, she thought about the story he had finally told her. She couldn't begin to imagine the horror he had gone through at losing his partner. She didn't want to think about the pain and guilt he had carried ever since. And she couldn't find the words to tell him how much it hurt to know everything he'd had to face.

All things she had to put behind her, too.

By the time the wedding reception ended on Friday night, she was both physically and mentally worn-out.

She sank onto a seat in the banquet hall and propped her feet up on the chair beside hers.

"Sandra made a beautiful bride," Tina said from two seats away.

"And a happy one," Jane admitted from the opposite side of the table. "I had my reservations, but everything all worked out. She ended up raving about every one of our services."

"I can't wait till we see Abuelo in the morning." Tina smiled. "He'll be so thrilled to know the wedding—"

"—went off without a hitch!" After chorusing his familiar phrase, all three of them burst into laughter.

"Really," Tina added, "you did a great job, Andi."

"We all did," she said. "It was a joint effort. Plus it was fun."

"And look at it this way," Jane said, "after you-know-who, any other event here ought to be a piece of cake."

They all laughed again.

"I'm going to take these platters to the kitchen," Tina said. "See you in the morning." She headed out of the banquet hall ahead of Andi and Jane, who rose more slowly to follow her.

"It must be a relief to feel you're off the hook." Jane smiled. "Since you agreed to stand in as planner only for this first wedding, you are now free."

"Yes." Free to move on. Free to leave Cowboy Creek. Free to walk away from Mitch. This time, forever.

## Chapter Nineteen

Mitch stepped into the Hitching Post's lobby and saw just the woman he wanted to see.

Andi was standing near the reception desk talking to Tina, who stood in her office doorway. Even as he froze, his training kicked in. He saw the new wreath on the front of the desk and the garland draped along the edges. He noted the rows of Christmas cards hung from strings across the wall behind the desk.

In the same swift glance, he took in Tina's welcoming smile and Andi's apprehensive expression. A second later, he felt the tightness in his chest when she looked away.

"Well, you're an early bird," Tina said with a laugh. "I'm not sure Abuela even has the coffee going yet. I'll go check."

Mitch held up a hand. "That's okay. I'm only here for a few minutes."

Tina nodded. "Then I'll get back to work." She went into her office behind the reception desk.

He looked at Andi and tilted his head toward the empty sitting room. "Got a few minutes?"

Andi nodded, and he followed her into the room. There were changes in here, too, a stuffed snowman standing in one corner and a ceramic Santa-driven sleigh and reindeer prancing across the mantel. On the shelf beside the chime clock sat a wooden donkey with a tilted sombrero and a red Christmas bow.

He smiled. "Looks good up there."

"I had to put him out of Trey's reach." She took a seat on one of the couches.

He stood near the fireplace and counted reindeer. "Looks like you've got a full crew."

She nodded. "Speaking of crew, we've got the waitresses who worked the reception last night coming in soon. Did you say you only had a few minutes?"

"Yeah. I'm headed to the sheriff's office to see my dad. I wanted to talk to him about a few things. And I wanted to run them by you, too."

She looked surprised, but said nothing.

"My appointment went well. I'll be going back to duty soon. And I have to admit, this enforced leave from the job has had its benefits. Besides getting to see you again, it's given me some time to think. Getting involved in the op in Arizona has done that, too. And now I hear my dad's planning on retiring. Everything coming together like this has helped me make some decisions."

Still no reaction. He pushed on. "There's going to be an opening for a deputy sheriff here in Cowboy Creek. And I intend to apply for it."

The positive reaction he had expected didn't come. Instead, her expression went completely blank, as if she couldn't summon politeness or even a passing interest. He couldn't take her silence. "No comment?"

"What do you want me to say?" She kept her voice low, but he could hear the repressed emotion. "I love you. You know that." She took a deep breath. "No matter what you think about my situation with Ginnie, that has nothing to do with what's between us, except for the fact that I *am* moving on."

"That's irony for you, isn't it? When I encouraged you to do that, I didn't mean away from me."

"I have to, Mitch, for my kids."

He took a half step toward her.

She shook her head. "Please don't. And if you've somehow tied us in to your decision to stay in Cowboy Creek, please don't do that, either. Don't make us your reason for giving up your job in LA." She stood and wrapped her arms around herself as if she'd felt a chill.

This time, he didn't move.

"I've told you how I feel about getting close to someone in a job like yours. I can't." Her voice broke. "I can't face the thought of Trey and Missy someday finding they've lost another daddy."

He stared silently at her. He had nothing more to say.

Andi stood frozen in place and watched Mitch turn and walk away. It broke her heart to see him go.

She wanted to change her mind. To call him back. To run to him and tell him—

Her thoughts were interrupted by a scream.

"Jed! *Dios mio—ayudame!*"

Andi started. The cries had come from the hallway leading to the kitchen.

The office door opened. "Abuela," Tina said in a hushed voice, her eyes wide. "She needs help."

Mitch was already across the lobby when Paz appeared in the doorway.

"Jed," she gasped. "On the floor. He won't wake up."

Mitch brushed past her and strode down the hall.

Paz followed. Andi rushed across the sitting room and ran behind Paz and Tina.

In the den, they found Jed sitting on the edge of the couch, flapping his hand as if to shoo Mitch away.

"I'm fine," he insisted. "Just had a weak spell. Nothing a drink of water won't cure."

"Sit back, Jed," Mitch said quietly. "You've got all the ladies worried. Let's just take a look to put their minds at ease."

From behind her, she heard running footsteps in the hallway. Robbie and Trey burst into the room.

Wide-eyed, Robbie gasped. "Grandpa's sick?"

"Sick?" Trey echoed.

"Grandpa's resting," Mitch said firmly. He made eye contact with Tina. "Didn't Pete say Daffodil was waiting to see the boys this morning?"

"Yes," she said quickly. "Yes, he did. Come on, you two, Abuelo's busy. We'll come back to see him after we visit Daffodil." With one hand on either boy's shoulder, she steered them from the room.

Mitch glanced over at Paz.

Andi looked in her direction, too. The older woman stood wringing her hands and staring at Jed.

"How about a glass of orange juice for this guy, Paz," Mitch suggested.

She nodded. "Yes, I'll bring it right away."

He had said just the right thing. Giving Paz something to do in her kitchen would calm her.

"Andi, could you call for an ambulance?"

*"Ambulance?"* Jed roared as Mitch pulled the afghan from the back of the couch and draped it around his shoulders. "Don't you do it, girl. I don't need an ambulance."

She was relieved to hear the strength in his voice, but wasn't about to give in to the demand.

As she crossed to the desk, Mitch said evenly, "Jed. Paz found you out cold on the floor. If the situation were reversed, you would want reassurance. Your family deserves that, too."

Jed glowered at her. She reached for the phone.

"I trust Mitch, Grandpa. If he thinks you need to get checked out at the hospital, I'm calling for the ambulance."

ANDI KEPT A close eye on Jed as he ate from the tray table pulled up to his hospital bed. "You make sure you finish every bite," she told him.

"I'm your granddaddy, not one of your kids," he grumbled.

But at the twinkle in his eye, she sighed in relief. She would never forget that ride in the ambulance Mitch had convinced Jed to take to the hospital.

Thanks heavens, his episode had turned out to be short-lived, stemming from a case of vertigo and a missed meal.

"I just can't believe you skipped dinner last night, Grandpa. Everyone might have been busy serving at the reception, but if you felt hungry, you should have raided the refrigerator."

He shrugged. "With all you women running in and out, it was more than my life was worth to set foot in that kitchen."

Tears sprang to her eyes. "Don't say that!"

Sheepishly, he patted her hand. "And don't you take on, girl. It's just an expression."

"One I don't ever want to hear again."

"You won't." He pushed the empty tray aside. "But I make no guarantees about what you'll hear if a doctor walks in here. I don't know why they feel the need to lock me up in this place overnight."

"It's just for observation. They want to make sure

you're hydrated properly before they send you home in the morning. You know that."

"A beer in Paz's kitchen would do me just fine."

"Oh, Grandpa," she said, laughing weakly and shaking her head.

The scare this morning could have been so much worse. Jed could have been facing a more serious condition. He could have hurt himself when he'd fallen to the floor. He could have passed out while Mitch wasn't around to take charge and counter all Jed's arguments.

As if he had read her thoughts, he said, "That young man of yours certainly knows his mind."

He wasn't her young man. Her fiancé. Her anything. She forced a light tone. "Sounds like some other bull-headed man I know."

He attempted to glare at her, but his lips twitched in a smile.

This morning, once they had arrived at the hospital and she had been reassured Jed was in good health, her thoughts turned to Mitch again and again.

He cared about Jed. About her. He was so good with the kids. As Grandpa had once said, he would make a good daddy someday. She already knew he was a wonderful lover.

But his choice of career—what he did, who he was—meant he could never be the man for her.

As tears sprang to her eyes again, she made a pretense of straightening the hospital sheets.

She had watched Mitch in action, calming everyone down and quietly taking control of the situation. Today, he had been her hero.

"What else is on your mind?" Jed asked quietly.

"Grandpa... Mitch and I aren't really engaged." She sighed. She hadn't planned to tell him this way, but she couldn't keep up the pretense any longer. And she had a feeling Jed had suspected all along.

He sat back and rested his folded his hands on the sheet, as if settling in for a long chat. "I'd guess there's more to the story than that."

Vainly, she tried to decide the best way to handle this conversation.

As if he had seen the struggle in her face, he said, "You know how I like to hear my news, girl. Flat-out straight."

Her laugh ended on a sob. His familiar phrase always made her smile, but she'd never heard him say it so gently.

She gave him a shorter version of what she had told Mitch about her worries over Grant's family, and especially her concerns about Ginnie. She left out the arguments Mitch had used to convince her to accept his idea, but confessed what they had hoped to do by pretending to be engaged.

"Your hearts were in the right place, I'll give you that," he said. "Family's important, more important than the two of you probably know yet. Look at what we've lost in the past few years, Andi. Not having your mama and your husband with us is sad enough. And look at how the rest of us have all grown apart. Time and distance both take their toll. It's important to keep in touch. To stay close."

She blinked hard to hold back a rush of tears. "You're right, Grandpa. And of course, I want to stay in touch with Ginnie. I'm planning to tell her exactly what I told you. I just wanted to help her and the rest of the family forget their grief and move on."

"Then you can, too."

*You're not willing to take your own advice and move on.*

Mitch's words hurt as much now as they had then.

"You already know this," Jed continued gruffly. "I'll say it, anyway. Life's too short not to keep moving while you've got the chance."

Blinking back tears, she nodded.

ANDI TOOK ONE last glance into the dresser mirror. Her gold-spangled party dress had looked great on the hanger but did nothing to make her feel ready for a party. She smoothed her hair, tried to soften the frown lines in her forehead and plastered a smile on her face.

Quickly turning from the mirror, she left the bedroom and went down the hall to Ginnie's room. She tapped on the door and waited till Ginnie called for her to come in. Her mother-in-law, in a tea-length red dress, stood in front of her own mirror.

"You look great," Andi said.

"And you look beautiful."

"Do you have a few minutes to talk before we go downstairs?"

"Well, of course. Come and sit." Ginnie took a seat on the chair near the window. "Did you get Missy up from her nap?"

"Yes. She's already downstairs." She crossed the room to sit on the edge of the bed.

"Good. Since Jed and I started taking turns holding Missy all day, I'm afraid we've made things harder for you with her nap schedule. Between the two of us, we have her spoiled. But that's what grandparents are for, isn't it?"

"Yes, it is. I'm glad you're getting the chance to do that this week. With me working and now with Missy and Trey and I all staying here at the ranch, I know you don't get to see the kids as much as you'd like."

"That's true. Although even if you were all living with

me, the way you and Grant did for a while, I don't think I could get enough of having you around."

"I know. We're your connection to him."

"You're all much more than that, Andi. Yes, Grant lives on through the children, but they're also the next generation, both of the Price family and my own. And you..." She smiled. "You're the daughter I always wanted."

Andi's throat tightened. At that moment, she couldn't respond. Fortunately, she didn't need to.

"I remember the day Grant brought you home to meet us," Ginnie continued. "I knew right away you were special to him, and that made you special to me. That's why it worries me to see you upset. There's been something bothering you, hasn't there?"

She nodded and gripped the edge of the bed on either side of her. "I...I have a confession to make. Mitch and I aren't really engaged."

Pursing her mouth, her mother-in-law nodded. "I wondered, when you two were 'old friends' at my house one night and then making your announcement two days later. And when, on the night between at Trey's party here, you didn't look like a couple who had just gotten engaged."

"I'm sorry." Sighing, she braced herself for what else she had to say. "I wish I could tell you I didn't plan to deceive you—or anyone—by pretending to be engaged. If it's any consolation, I was trying to keep you from getting hurt."

"It looks to me like you were the one hurt in the process," Ginnie said sadly. "But why would you think I'd be hurt to see you happy again?"

"It wasn't that." Haltingly, she explained, keeping the focus on her need to take care of her kids. "I want to be able to support them myself."

"And knowing you, I wouldn't expect anything less. You're a terrific mother. Of course you would want to take care of Trey and Missy, to put them first in your life, as you should."

"Thank you. But it's more than that," she went on. "I need to be independent for my own sake, too. The kids and I love you, Ginnie. And you've always been there for me. But I feel if you continue to be there for me, I won't learn to stand on my own."

Ginnie smiled wryly. "Are you suggesting I drop you from the family tree?"

"No." She laughed. "But maybe let me go out on a limb once in a while."

"And this is why you felt the need for your so-called engagement?"

Silently, she nodded.

Ginnie came to sit beside her. She shook Andi's arm gently. "I need to knock some sense into you, as Jed would say. You're putting a roof over your family's head and raising your children—my grandchildren—all by yourself. How much more independent can you be?"

"I don't know." She flushed. "Sometimes, I just feel that I need to…"

"Cut the cord to the Price family?"

Again, she couldn't respond. She had never felt so tongue-tied or as sure of ruining a situation as she did this one.

"When I first married," Ginnie continued, "there were times I felt the same way."

"There were?"

She nodded. "Being a Price is a privilege, but it also carries obligations. It wasn't long after I married into the family that I went looking for some independence, too.

"And I got lucky."

Andi blinked. "How?" She was fascinated by this new view of her mother-in-law.

"Eventually, I managed to find my independence and my niche *within* the family." She smiled. "That's my solution, not yours. I knew you would have to find your independence on the outside. And you already have."

Her throat tightened again, but she managed to blurt her thanks. Mitch had been right, after all, as Ginnie's obvious concern for her proved.

"But, Andi," she said gently, "though you're on your own now, you'll never *be* alone. Through Trey and Missy, your link to me is as strong as the bond you share with Jed. We're all *family*. And we all love one another." She wrapped her arm around Andi's shoulders and gave her a quick hug.

"I know life's not always the way we want it to be," she went on. "And I realize life may take you farther from me in miles than you are now. But can we make a deal?"

"Of course."

"Good." Ginnie smiled. "As for my not seeing the kids as much as I like… I'll be honest, twenty-four hours a day wouldn't be enough. But whenever I *am* able to see you and the kids, promise you'll let me spoil them just a bit. And when I can't see you all, I promise to do only a little grumbling."

Andi laughed. "All right, that's a deal."

"Good," Ginnie said again. "Now, since I'm leaving for home in the morning, let's go find a couple of grandkids for me to spoil."

# Chapter Twenty

Andi stood beside Jed in the hotel lobby to greet their guests for the open house. She, Tina and Jane had all assured Paz they would take turns staying by his side.

He seemed as healthy and steady as Andi had ever seen him and twice as energetic while he talked about hosting the party. But Paz, who was busy running her kitchen, was worried about him overdoing it.

The front door swung open, pushing a drift of early-evening air into the lobby. When Andi saw who had stepped through the door, she felt grateful for the cool breeze.

As she watched Mitch make his way toward them, she held Jed's arm—not because he seemed unsteady but because she needed to brace herself. The Weston family had arrived earlier, and though her heart had plummeted when she saw Mitch wasn't with them, she had told herself it was for the best.

As he reached them, her heartbeat seemed to flicker like the twinkling lights on the Christmas tree.

He smiled at her, then reached to shake hands with Jed. "They let you out already. I can see why. You're looking good."

"I'm feeling even better. Must be all this clean living

and a clear conscience. Which is more than I can say for you, after that stunt you pulled about your engagement."

*"Grandpa."* She was grateful for the voices and laughter all around them. "Please don't blame Mitch. It was my decision. He was only trying to help me."

"Some help." Despite his gruff tone, she could see the loving concern in his eyes.

"It was my idea," Mitch said just as stubbornly as he had the morning they had returned from Santa Fe. "I'm as much at fault for this, if not more."

"Either way," Jed said, "seems like neither of you did a good job of sticking to your plan."

She flushed. "No, we didn't."

He stared at them both for a long moment, then patted her arm. "Well, I'll be off. Someone's got to be the life of this party, and I'm sure you two have some talking to do."

"Oh, but, Grandpa—"

"Calm down, girl. Tina's just three yards north of us. I'll go take my turn standing with her now."

Swallowing a laugh, she watched him walk away.

"Do we?" Mitch asked.

She started. "What?"

"Have some talking to do."

She took a deep breath. "Yes, I think we do."


MITCH FOLLOWED ANDI up the stairs, knowing she was leading him to the suite the women had been using for the wedding preparations.

The overhead hall light struck her gold dress, making it sparkle, but he had already been dazzled by her the moment he'd seen her standing in the lobby.

In the suite, a mountain of paperwork still covered the bed. She pushed some of it aside and took a seat. Mitch remained by the closed door.

She linked her fingers and took a deep breath. "I'm glad you're here tonight. I was so busy with Grandpa yesterday, I never even thanked you for everything."

"I don't need any thanks. That's part of what I do."

"Be a hero."

"I'm nobody's hero, Andi. I'm just me. I sure found that out recently." He shook his head, ashamed at how long it had taken him to discover the truth.

"Tell me," she said softly.

Why was it so hard to do just that, to tell her he'd received as much help from her as he had tried to give? He sighed. "Look, I already explained I don't do feelings. I've also always refused to let anything get to me, always thought I was invincible, I guess. What happened brought me to my knees, literally. That's what taught me there aren't any guarantees in life. And it tore me up with guilt. Not just over my partner, though that was most of it."

He crossed to the desk and took a seat close to her. He didn't want to share the admission he was about to make, but if that was the road to progress, he was taking it.

"After the incident, I believed I'd let down my family, too. My dad was always my hero. So was my granddad. You know he was on the force, too, before he retired?"

"Yes. I remember. You once told me that was why you wanted to become a cop. Because of them."

He nodded. "That was partly it. Law enforcement is in my blood. It's the only job I want to do. And I felt I let down my family and myself by not being the cop I should have been."

"You weren't at fault."

"I know. Now. You helped me see I couldn't have out-talked a fellow cop who was following his own gut feeling, especially when he pulled rank. It was a hell of a way for me to confirm I can trust my own instincts, too."

He smiled briefly. "But I *can* trust them, especially the one telling me to take the job with the sheriff's department. What happened with Jed yesterday proved that to me. I didn't become a cop for the thrill or danger of the job, but to serve and protect. Becoming a town sheriff satisfies that need.

"As for my other needs…" He ran his fingertips down her cheek. "Andi, no woman but you will ever satisfy me. And I want to live the rest of my life right here—with you and our kids."

"Mitch—"

"Don't say it, please. I know how you feel about my job, but Cowboy Creek is a much safer place than LA to raise a family." He held her gaze. "I'm not going anywhere, no matter what. And I'll wait, no matter how long it takes you to feel ready to go forward with me. And if you're never ready, I'll still be waiting."

She sighed.

His heart missed a few beats.

Then she gave him a small smile. "While you were gone, I took your advice. I did a lot of thinking. And after you became *our hero*," she said firmly, "I thought some more. And you're right—there are no guarantees. I learned that with Grant. With my mom. On that ride in the ambulance with Grandpa. And when I thought I'd lost you—again."

He smiled. "Sounds to me like we've made some progress on both sides."

"We have. And I'm thankful you're taking the job here in Cowboy Creek, for all the reasons you said." She touched his cheek. "You're a good cop, Mitch, and a wonderful man. And we've postponed our happy-ever-after long enough. I'm ready *now*. For always."

He got down on his knee beside the bed and pulled a small white box from his pocket.

"Oh, no," she cried in mock disappointment. "You're not letting me choose my own ring?"

"Where's the romance in that?" He tucked a strand of her hair behind her ear just for the chance to touch her again. "I love you. I always have."

Her eyes glistened.

He flicked open the jewel box and showed her the ring inside, a diamond offset by two small blue sapphires. "You're the diamond in the middle, Andi, and Missy and Trey are the stones on either side." He slid the ring onto her finger. "I love you all. Will you marry me?"

"Will you serve and protect us?"

"You know I will."

"Will you love, honor and cherish us?"

"I already do."

"I already do, too, Mitch. You know that."

"Yes, I do. But this engagement won't be official until you give me your answer."

She laughed. He reached up to brush a tear from her cheek. "Yes," she said. "We'll marry you."

# Epilogue

*Christmas morning*

His arm around Andi, Mitch stood near the Christmas tree in the Hitching Post's sitting room. They had been engaged—for real, this time—for all of a day, and already he knew he was part of the Garland clan.

Jed grinned at him from his seat near the fireplace. "I gather you'll be here for Paz's Christmas dinner this afternoon."

Mitch held Andi more snugly against him. "I plan to be around for all the holiday dinners from now on."

"And you're really taking a deputy's job in town?" Jane asked.

"If they'll have me."

"Oh, they will," Jed promised. "I've got an in with the sheriff."

Paz set a glass on the small table by Jed's elbow. "You forgot this in the dining room."

"Don't fuss, woman," he snapped. But he smiled up at her before taking a big gulp of water.

He looked around the room at his family. Mitch could see the tears in his eyes. "You girls have made me proud," Jed said gruffly. "The Hitching Post has been put on the

map, with the first wedding going off without a hitch…
so to speak."

All three of the man's granddaughters laughed.
Jed grinned at them. "I've outdone myself with this
final matchmaking assignment, if I do say so myself.
And thanks to Tina and Cole, I'm going to be a great-
granddaddy once again." He nodded in satisfaction.
"Darned good work, for an old man with a dream."

Mitch knew not one of them in the room could dis-
agree.

He had a lot to be thankful for, too.

His parents had been solidly behind his decision to
apply for a deputy's position. He had talked to his dad
at the office, as he had told Andi he would. But first he
had spoken to his mom.

*Nothing will make your dad happier than knowing
you're joining the department, too.*

*And you?*

*Sweetheart, you know I just want whatever will make
you happy.*

Coming home to Andi and the kids…to his families,
old and new…to a job in Cowboy Creek… All that fit
the bill.

He even felt thankful for Jed's matchmaking scheme.

And when his bride-to-be led him to the sitting room
door and the dangling sprig of mistletoe, he knew right
down to his bones he was exactly where he belonged.

\* \* \* \* \*

## #1577 THE COWBOY'S CONVENIENT BRIDE
### by Donna Alward

When Tanner Hudson proposes to new mom Laura Jessup, he's just trying to protect her. But the more he gets to know Laura, the more Tanner wants her to be his bride for real.

## #1578 THE TEXAS RANGER'S NANNY
### *Lone Star Lawmen*
### by Rebecca Winters

Widower Texas Ranger Vic Malone hires Claire Ames to care for seven-year-old Jeremy, not knowing how important she will turn out to be in the most important case he's ever worked on—finding his son.

## #1579 THE BABY AND THE COWBOY SEAL
### *Cowboy SEALs*
### by Laura Marie Altom

Navy SEAL Wiley James has returned to his family ranch a broken man. He just wants to be left alone, but single mom Macy Shelton—who's had a crush on Wiley her whole life—has other plans!

## #1580 TWINS FOR THE REBEL COWBOY
### *The Boones of Texas*
### by Sasha Summers

Annabeth Upton finally has her life on track after her husband's death. Then an unexpected encounter with Ryder Boone results in Annabeth expecting twins! Can she find happiness a second time around?

---

# REQUEST YOUR FREE BOOKS!
## 2 FREE NOVELS PLUS 2 FREE GIFTS!

 HARLEQUIN®

# American Romance®

## LOVE, HOME & HAPPINESS

**YES!** Please send me 2 FREE Harlequin® American Romance® novels and my 2 FREE gifts (gifts are worth about $10). After receiving them, if I don't wish to receive any more books, I can return the shipping statement marked "cancel." If I don't cancel, I will receive 4 brand-new novels every month and be billed just $4.74 per book in the U.S. or $5.49 per book in Canada. That's a savings of at least 12% off the cover price! It's quite a bargain! Shipping and handling is just 50¢ per book in the U.S. and 75¢ per book in Canada.* I understand that accepting the 2 free books and gifts places me under no obligation to buy anything. I can always return a shipment and cancel at any time. Even if I never buy another book, the two free books and gifts are mine to keep forever.

154/354 HDN GHZZ

| | | |
|---|---|---|
| Name | (PLEASE PRINT) | |
| Address | | Apt. # |
| City | State/Prov. | Zip/Postal Code |

Signature (if under 18, a parent or guardian must sign)

### Mail to the **Reader Service:**
**IN U.S.A.:** P.O. Box 1867, Buffalo, NY 14240-1867
**IN CANADA:** P.O. Box 609, Fort Erie, Ontario L2A 5X3

**Want to try two free books from another line?**
**Call 1-800-873-8635 or visit www.ReaderService.com.**

\* Terms and prices subject to change without notice. Prices do not include applicable taxes. Sales tax applicable in N.Y. Canadian residents will be charged applicable taxes. Offer not valid in Quebec. This offer is limited to one order per household. Not valid for current subscribers to Harlequin American Romance books. All orders subject to credit approval. Credit or debit balances in a customer's account(s) may be offset by any other outstanding balance owed by or to the customer. Please allow 4 to 6 weeks for delivery. Offer available while quantities last.

**Your Privacy**—The Reader Service is committed to protecting your privacy. Our Privacy Policy is available online at www.ReaderService.com or upon request from the Reader Service.

We make a portion of our mailing list available to reputable third parties that offer products we believe may interest you. If you prefer that we not exchange your name with third parties, or if you wish to clarify or modify your communication preferences, please visit us at www.ReaderService.com/consumerschoice or write to us at Reader Service Preference Service, P.O. Box 9062, Buffalo, NY 14240-9062. Include your complete name and address.

HARI5

SPECIAL EXCERPT FROM

# HARLEQUIN®

# American Romance®

*Tanner Hudson and Laura Jessup have made
a lot of mistakes. Can a marriage of convenience be
the answer to both their problems?*

*Read on for a sneak preview of*
**THE COWBOY'S CONVENIENT BRIDE**
*by Donna Alward.*

"Doesn't it bother you?" she asked bluntly. "What they say about me?"

His eyes darkened. "You mean about Rowan's father?"

Laura nodded, nerves jumping around in her stomach. He was the first person she'd broached the topic with, and she realized that for whatever reason, she trusted him.

"It's none of my business," he stated, not unkindly. "And believe me, Laura, after all these years, I know what it's like to have to live with mistakes. And live them down."

"You?" Granted, she'd heard he was a bit of a player, but if that was the worst anyone said about him…

"Right. You were gone for a while, so maybe you don't know. I was married once. For three whole days. In Vegas. The entire town knows about it. My best man at the time wasn't discreet with the details."

She blinked. "You were married for three days?"

"Yeah. Until we both sobered up and she came to her senses. You don't have the corner on mistakes, Laura, and I certainly have no right to judge anyone. So no, what they say doesn't bother me."

Tanner leaned forward and placed a chaste, but soft, kiss on her cheek. "Take care and thanks again for dinner."

"You're welcome. And thank you for everything today." She smiled. "You're starting to become my knight in shining armor."

He laughed. "Oh, hardly. Just being neighborly. Anyone else would have done the same." He raised his hand in farewell. "See you around."

He fired up his truck and drove away, leaving Laura back in reality again. But it was a softer kind of reality, because for the first time in a long while, it felt as if someone might be in her corner.

And she truly hadn't realized how lonely she'd become until someone walked in and brought sunshine with him. Tanner had said that anyone would have done the same, but she knew that was a lie. She'd been in that parking lot for a good half hour with the hood up before he came along to help. Others had passed right on by.

It was just too bad that Tanner Hudson was the last person she should get involved with. Even if Maddy was gracious enough to understand, she knew the town of Gibson never would.

*Don't miss*
**THE COWBOY'S CONVENIENT BRIDE**
*by Donna Alward,*
*available in January 2016 wherever*
*Harlequin® American Romance®*
*books and ebooks are sold.*

www.Harlequin.com

# HARLEQUIN®

A *Romance* FOR EVERY MOOD™

# JUST CAN'T GET ENOUGH?

Join our social communities
and talk to us online.

You will have access to the latest
news on upcoming titles and special
promotions, but most importantly,
you can talk to other fans about your
favorite Harlequin reads.

Harlequin.com/Community

 Facebook.com/HarlequinBooks

 Twitter.com/HarlequinBooks

Pinterest.com/HarlequinBooks

# THE WORLD IS BETTER WITH

*Romance*

Harlequin has everything from contemporary, passionate and heartwarming to suspenseful and inspirational stories.

Whatever your mood, we have a romance just for you!

Connect with us to find your next great read, special offers and more.

**f** /HarlequinBooks

**🐦** @HarlequinBooks

www.HarlequinBlog.com

www.Harlequin.com/Newsletters